What Do You Believe In?

Work. Love. Religion.

Robert Makula

contained within this document, including, but not limited to, errors, omissions, or inaccuracies.

Table of Contents

INTRODUCTION 1

WALK WITH ME 1

   One Step at a Time 2

CHAPTER 1: WHY ARE YOU IMPORTANT?..................................3

YOUR IMPORTANCE TO THE WORLD..4

   You Are Alive 4

   Your Life Has a Purpose 5

   Share Your Wisdom 6

   You Are Special 7

BELIEVING THAT YOU ARE IMPORTANT 8

   Confidence Boosters 9

   Rebuilding Lost Confidence 11

CHAPTER 2: UNDERSTANDING BELIEF.....................................13

WHAT IS BELIEF? 14

   Belief Systems..14

   What Do People Believe In? 15

   Why Does It Matter What You Believe? 16

   What Should You Believe in? 17

READY. SET. GO! 20

CHAPTER 3: ANALYZING BELIEFS 21

CORE BELIEFS..22

   Where Do Beliefs Come From? 23

   The Nitty Gritty Side of Core Beliefs..26

ARE BELIEFS WORTH CHANGING? 27

   Should Beliefs Be Changed? 29

   Upgrading Beliefs 29

CHAPTER 4: UNDERSTANDING RELIGION: DIFFERENT RELIGIONS 33

WHAT IS RELIGION? 34

   Definition of Religion 35

EXPLORING DIFFERENT RELIGIONS 35

   Islam 36

Judaism...*39*

Christianity *42*

Other Religions *46*

CHAPTER 5: UNDERSTANDING RELIGION: THE UPS AND DOWNS OF RELIGION49

THE PROS AND CONS OF RELIGION 50

It's All About God..*50*

The Cons of Believing in Religion *51*

The Pros of Believing in Religion *52*

ENDING ON A HIGH NOTE..54

CHAPTER 6: THE POWER OF LOVE **57**

WHAT IS LOVE?...58

Different Types of Love..*58*

The Importance of Trust in a Relationship......................................*60*

Telltale Signs of a Healthy, Trustworthy Relationship *62*

EMOTIONAL INTELLIGENCE: THE ADVANTAGES AND DISADVANTAGES...........63

Advantages of Emotional Intelligence..*64*

Disadvantages of Emotional Intelligence *65*

IN SUMMARY 67

What Makes Love Important?..*68*

CHAPTER 7: LIVING IN A WORLD THAT IS DRIVEN BY STATUS **69**

THE IMPORTANCE OF STATUS IN OUR LIVES 70

Status: Through the Eyes of the World..*70*

Status: It Is Not Optional *71*

Status: Positive Changes...*72*

THE DOWNSIDE OF BEING DRIVEN BY STATUS 72

Bad Decisions *72*

Keeping up With the Joneses...*73*

Double-Sided Religious Sword *74*

CHAPTER 8: FOR THE LOVE OF WORK **75**

THE IMPORTANCE OF WORKING 75

Finances..*76*

Climbing the Ladder of Success *76*

Distraction..*77*

Character...*77*

Respect..*77*

YOUR CAREER IS YOUR WHOLE WORLD: PROS AND CONS 77

Stacking the Pros *78*

Unpacking the Cons..*80*

DO NOT COMPROMISE YOUR BELIEFS FOR YOUR CAREER 82

Signs of Idolizing Your Job *83*

CHAPTER 9: FOR THE LOVE OF MONEY **85**

THE IMPORTANCE OF HAVING MONEY 87
MONEY: THE GOOD AND THE BAD 87
For the Good of Money..*88*
For the Bad of Money *88*
ALLOWING MONEY TO COMPROMISE BELIEFS 89
Losing Sight of God..*90*
Do Not Lose Sight of Yourself *91*

CHAPTER 10: FINDING THE GOOD IN YOUR HABITUAL LIFESTYLE...............**93**

RE-EVALUATING GOALS 94
S.M.A.R.T Goals Concept *94*
Goal Problems *95*
Examples of Goals *96*
HOW DO HABITS AFFECT YOUR LIFE? 96
Advantages and Disadvantages of Developing Habits...............*97*
Re-Defining Your Habits to Improve Your Life *98*
Turn Your Back on Bad Habits *100*

CHAPTER 11: OBSERVING LIFESTYLE CHOICES: DIET AND EXERCISE...............**101**

DIET: WHEN THE LOVE OF FOOD BECOMES AN OBSESSION 102
Do Not Judge a Book by Its Cover................................*102*
Pros and Cons of Dieting *103*
Food Scarcity Leads to Food Obsession *104*
All Your Hope Is in Food..*106*
FITNESS: WHEN THE LOVE OF EXERCISE BECOMES AN OBSESSION 107
When Fitness Becomes an Obsession...............................*107*
IN SUMMARY 108

CHAPTER 12: FOR THE BEAUTY OF SLEEP **109**

THE IMPORTANCE OF SLEEP 109
Benefits of a Good Night's Rest.................................*110*
Proposed Sleep Schedule *112*
Disorders That Interfere With Quality of Sleep..................*113*
Improving Quality of Sleep *114*
WHEN SLEEP BECOMES THE CENTER OF YOUR UNIVERSE.........................115
Too Much of a Good Thing Is Not Good *116*
When Sleep Becomes an Addiction *116*
IN SUMMARY 118

CHAPTER 13: CREATING NEW AND BEAUTIFUL MEMORIES...............**119**

LEARN FROM THE PAST AND BUILD A BRIGHTER FUTURE 120
It Is Your Story *120*

Acknowledge Your Mistakes..*121*

Learn From the Bad Experiences *121*

No Apology? Move along *122*

THE BENEFITS OF BEAUTIFUL MEMORIES *123*

Focus *123*

No One Can Hack Into Your Brain..*123*

CHAPTER 14: CREATING YOUR TAILORMADE LIFESTYLE: ONE PIECE AT A TIME
....**125**

MAKULA BANK OF BELIEFS...*126*

Recovering Your Lost Beliefs..*126*

Believe in Yourself *127*

SOUL SEARCHING: DIGGING DEEP TO FIND YOUR PURPOSE IN LIFE *129*

Why Should You Search Your Soul? *129*

Searching Your Soul...*130*

IN SUMMARY *131*

CHAPTER 15: CREATING YOUR TAILORMADE LIFESTYLE: PUTTING THE PIECES TOGETHER **133**

APPLYING YOUR BELIEFS...*134*

Beliefs Refresher...*135*

Analysis and Application of Beliefs *135*

STRENGTHS AND WEAKNESSES OF BELIEF *136*

Signs That You Are Strong In Your Beliefs...*137*

Signs That You Are Weak In Your Beliefs *138*

CREATING A BALANCED LIFESTYLE *139*

Structure of Balance *139*

CHAPTER 16: BUILDING THE BRIDGE: CROSSING IT WITH SELF-CONFIDENCE .**141**

CONFIDENCE AND BELIEF: THE HUNT BEGINS *142*

Switching Negativity With Positivity *142*

Overcome Biggest Fears..*143*

Pay Attention to the Solution, Not the Problem *143*

Other Self-Help Tips...*143*

HAVING THE CONFIDENCE TO MAKE CHOICES THAT BENEFIT YOUR BELIEFS *144*

No Doubts..*145*

At Peace With Your Choice *145*

The Necessity of Choices...*145*

The More You Choose, the More Choices Are Made *146*

HAVING THE CONFIDENCE TO BOUNCE BACK FROM MISGUIDED CHOICES......................*146*

Emotional *147*

Fact Check *147*

Listen to Your Inner Voice...*147*

CHAPTER 17: LIFE LESSONS: LEARNING FROM MISTAKES.............................149

THE NO JUDGMENT POLICY 150
LIFE LESSONS: UNDERSTANDING THE DIFFERENT TYPES OF MISTAKES...........................151
  Mistakes by Other People..151
  Standard Mistakes..151
  Silly Mistakes..152
  Warning Mistakes...152
  Necessary Mistakes..152
  Mistakes in Summary..153
LIFE LESSONS: DO NOT LET FEAR HOLD YOU BACK.....................................153
  Positive Affirmations...154

CHAPTER 18: TRUST YOURSELF BY BEING BRAVE, WISE, AND THE PERSON YOU WANT TO BE 157

TRUST..158
  Be Who You Need to Be—Yourself 158
  Setting and Keeping Goals...158
  Kindness and Strength..159
BRAVERY 159
  Facing Our Fears...160
  Stand Up for What You Believe In 161
BE WHO YOU ARE MEANT TO BE 161
  Priorities Change 162
  Dealing With Issues...162
  Cut the Negative Out of Your Life...................................163
THE END IS WITHIN REACH 163

CHAPTER 19: YOU ARE UNIQUE: ACCEPT AND EMBRACE WHO YOU ARE........165

IMPORTANCE OF SELF-AWARENESS 166
  Benefits of Self-Awareness 166
ACCEPTING AND EMBRACING YOUR SELF-AWARENESS 168
  The Importance of Self-Care..168
  Listen to Your Gut...168
  Be Positive 169

CHAPTER 20: I BELIEVE IN YOU, SO YOU NEED TO BELIEVE IN YOU 171

WHY IS BELIEVING IN YOURSELF SO IMPORTANT?.....................172
  Who Is Going to Believe in You if You Do Not Believe in Yourself?............172
  Be Confident in Confidence..172
  You Are Your Own Inspiration 173
  You Failed: Every Cloud Has a Silver Lining.....................173
ONCE UPON A TIME..174

CONCLUSION **177**

   The Last Word *177*

REFERENCES...**179**

Introduction

During our journey through life, we encounter many crossroads. At each of these crossroads, we have to decide which direction to take. The journey is not as easy as we would like it to be. Life presents us with many obstacles. We question these obstacles because they are not what we envisioned. Work. Health. Finances. Relationships. Family. Beliefs. Faith. We might never have all the answers as to why these obstacles are placed before us, but we can try to understand why they might be there.

Before I knew God, there was the only person I knew—me. After much soul-searching, I realized that God was there before me and the people I surrounded myself with. Growing up, I was angry at the world. I was especially angry with God until I realized that my soul was not with God. I was a lost soul.

Continuing on my soul-searching quest, I gave my heart to God and asked Him to fill me with the Holy Spirit. My eyes were opened, my soul was filled with the Spirit, and today, I am flying high on the wings of the eagle. I found my soul thanks to my belief in God. I am no longer a lost soul walking around filled with anger. Thanks to my newfound faith, my heart was and is still bursting with the love I have for my Savior.

Walk With Me

I wanted to write this book to show people that they are not lost causes, and that no matter what their situations are, it is never too late to find peace. Yes, there are crossroads and we are at a loss of which direction we should take, but with God or any other deity in our lives, we choose a direction that is based on our faith or belief systems.

I want to introduce you to yourself. I want to help you understand where you are in your life journey. I will attempt to answer questions you have been asking yourself, and give you a clearer understanding of what may or may not be important to you. This is your journey of self-discovery. You will not be bullied, nor will you be judged. This is an opportunity for you to move forward in your life, instead of trying to right the wrongs of your past. As much as you want to change the past, it is impossible because you cannot turn back the clock. Instead, you are going to learn how to shape your future.

One Step at a Time

It is time to get comfortable with your book or digital device. Take all the time you need to digest everything; there is no rush and no time limit. You set the pace at which you are comfortable. Together we will embark on this journey one step at a time, and by the time you reach the end, you will know which direction your heart needs to go. There will be no judgment and no bullying. This book is all about you and your choices for the next crossroads in your life.

Chapter 1:

Why Are You Important?

A family member tells you that you are important to them and that they would not be able to live without you. The very next day, that same family member makes a hurtful comment and does not speak to you for weeks. Why say that you are important when the actions do not convey the statement?

You have a good job, and your supervisors or management sing your praises. You are floating on cloud nine because you know you are important to the company. A month later, you are handed a letter stating that your services are no longer required. You believed that you were important to the company. Why praise you for your work, and then terminate your contract if it was implied that you were important to the company?

Everyone has gone through periods in their lives where things do not go according to plan. It seems as if the odds are against you. There are times that you feel as if you are in a hole, and the harder you try to dig yourself out, the deeper the hole becomes. You feel as if you are the only one going through hardships. The walls are closing in around you, suffocating you, and you are feeling overwhelmed. You have tried to reach out to those closest to you for support, but you are feeling as if you are not being heard. You are doubting everyone. You do not trust anyone, and you feel as if everyone is against you. People tell you that you are important to them, but you do not believe them. Why are you important when nothing seems to be going your way?

Your Importance to the World

You find it difficult to believe that you are important when you are faced with conflict, as is mentioned in the above scenarios. You doubt your importance in life. Why are you born into a world where you are struggling to understand your importance? Even though you doubt your importance, there are people in your life who value who you are. They might not express their feelings, but to them, you are important.

Your presence does not go unnoticed. If you go to the store or the local fast-food restaurant, and you smile at the person helping you, you are touching their hearts with your kindness. For all you know, your smile is what they need because they are having a difficult day. Still at the store, you encounter a customer who is trying to reach an item on the top shelf, and you step forward to take the item down for them. You are important to the customer because you showed kindness by being in the right place at the right time.

You Are Alive

You might be questioning your existence because right now, you are struggling to understand your purpose in life. The fact that you are alive and reading this proves that you are where you are meant to be. The sperm cell that fertilizes the egg to conceive you is evident that you are meant to be alive. You were handpicked to be born into this world.

Think of your body as if it is an unfurnished house. When you move into the house, you are tasked with furnishing it to make a home. You paint the walls, you decorate, and you fill it with memories. You make your home a safe haven for you and your family, even though there are no guarantees you will live in that home for the rest of your life.

As you grow, you are furnishing your home. You make your own decisions, you are responsible for your thoughts and actions. As you would do with a home, you will tire of the color of the paint, the decorations, or the way your furniture is placed. You will do a little home renovation to modernize.

In life, your priorities will change. What you chose to do as a child is not who you are today, nor will it be who you are in the future. Circumstances change so that we can grow and learn from our experiences. Nothing in life is guaranteed. The home you have lovingly furnished and decorated is not going to be there forever. However, the memories you made in that home will be preserved in your heart because it was important to you.

The day you die, you will leave your footprint in the lives of those you touched. Whether you want to believe it or not, because you were born and lived, you are important to many people whose path you crossed. It is never too late to make an impression on those around you. You are unique, there is only one of you in this world. Your existence is important. You are important.

Your Life Has a Purpose

Did you know that there are over seven billion people on this earth? Each one of those seven billion has a purpose in life. Whether you have touched someone's life by greeting them as you walk by, or helping someone who has no means to replace a broken fence, you have a purpose.

I recently heard a story about a middle-aged lady that is having problems with the electrical wiring in her home. Whenever it rained, her power went off. During the last rainy season, she had no electricity in a section of her home for approximately three months. She asked her friend, who is an electrician, for assistance in identifying the problem but the friend never came through for her, despite making promises. She never asked again and continued living with extension cables to power certain areas of her home.

After a year, this lady met a family in the community where she lives. The family needed her assistance and wanted to pay her for her help but she politely declined the payment. What happened after that was a rollercoaster ride for this lady. The family swooped in and started fixing small things around the house that had broken or needed replacing. While the electrical issue is still not addressed, and cannot be taken care of until the rainy season starts, the family had seen other more pressing issues that needed to be taken care of.

Everyone involved in this scenario had a purpose. Neither the lady or the family spoke about the good they did for each other. It is not advertised to the community. As for the friend, she continued making promises but did not follow through.

You do not need to be a multi-millionaire to have a purpose. You do not need to be someone famous. All you need is to identify what interests you. Think about something you are passionate about. Whether your passion is writing, gardening, cooking, reading, or spots, you can use it to help those around you. If you do not have any passions, consider exploring your options to find something that interests you, something you feel will help someone someday. Do something that you will be proud to tell your children or grandchildren that you did.

Regardless of what you believe, you do have a purpose. The family that stepped in to help the lady make repairs to her home has the purpose to help those less fortunate. The lady that declined payment for doing something good for the family has a purpose to help in ways that do not require financial assistance. Your purpose, however big or small, is important to someone.

Share Your Wisdom

No matter where you are currently in your journey through life, you have a story to share. Whether it is a childhood memory of learning how to fold laundry, or a teenage memory of trying alcohol for the first time, you learned something that you are able to share with someone. Your story could be what the person you are talking to needs to hear.

Whatever you have gone through or experienced until this present moment in your life, you have the wisdom to help someone else. When you are in the company of someone who is telling you about something they experienced, it might jar your memory into remembering a similar experience. There might be a painful memory of how you lost a beloved family member that you had suppressed that is suddenly triggered. You get to share your coping tools with others.

Sharing what you know may help others. If you think about the self-help books you read, the writer is sharing what they have learned with the world. If you are speaking to a friend or a stranger, you are sharing the knowledge of what you have experienced with them. The story you share about the day you got your first pet might seem insignificant to you. You might just be telling the person something they need to hear that confirms that they are making the right decision.

You are probably shaking your head while reading this, thinking that you do not have anything of value to share. Do not sell yourself short. Your wisdom and knowledge is important and it will add value to someone at some point during your life.

You Are Special

Every one of the over seven billion people on this earth is special. The day of your birth was a joyous event and celebrated by family, friends, and strangers. It is hard to believe that you are special, especially if you have doubts about yourself. No one knows what is happening in your mind, body, and soul. Not everyone is comfortable showing emotions. Some might consider you a hard nut to crack. This may be because you have been hurt by people you trusted.

I am here to tell you that you are special. You are unique; there is only one you. You appreciate people. You know, even though you deny it, that there are people that care about you. Share the love and appreciation in your heart with those around you. Little acts of kindness mean more than showering someone with a gift that will not be used. It is the little acts that draw people to you. Do not wait until it is too late to show people that you love and care about them.

Imagine a snow globe. You are on the outside looking in. Everyone you have ever crossed paths with during your life is living in the globe. You are not in there with them because your life ended abruptly. You can see friends and family crying or you see the homeless person you bought a meal for looking at a loss. You are special to everyone who you have ever encountered. They miss your presence in their lives. You brought something to their lives that made you unique.

You should not be someone you are not comfortable being. Be the person you are meant to be. Engrave your footprint in the hearts of those who matter. Whenever you are doubting yourself, look in the mirror and tell yourself that you are important to someone. Live up to your potential, not the potential society wants you to live up to. You are more important to the world than you realize or give yourself credit for.

Believing That You Are Important

In the previous section, you learned that you are important. You might not have agreed with some or all of the statements mentioned, but from an outsider's point of view, you are important to many people. You might still be digesting the fact that your existence puts a smile on the face of someone or that your "good morning" or "good afternoon" meant something significant to someone. This book is going to help you understand yourself, and what you mean to the world.

You chose this book because you want to learn something about yourself from an outsider's point of view. This book is not going to tell you what you should or should not be doing. You are not going to be forced into a corner where you will be tortured into making a decision. You want to understand what others see in you. You want to understand what your purpose in life is. Why should you have confidence, why should you believe, and why should you trust?

Not everything you will read will meet your expectations at that moment, and that is perfectly fine. By the time you read the end of this book, you will know what your purpose in life is and why you deserved to be on this earth.

This book is not going to discriminate against anyone. Every person on this earth deserves a piece of the ground they walk on. No one is going to be judged or bullied into believing one way or the other. This book is for everyone to ready, regardless of their age, race, sex, physical appearance, past, or the size of their bank balance. If you do not like anyone that falls into the examples mentioned, that is your personal choice. This book is going to change your views on how you view people, and you will learn how to tolerate everyone from all walks of life. If you are feeling lost, have low self-esteem, or distrust everyone, imagine that others are going through what you are.

I have been where you are. I have allowed my anger, resentment, and insecurity to consume my life. I have doubted myself. I have battled with my confidence for as long as I can remember. In my darkest hour, I chose to look for God. I opened my heart and allowed Him in. I believed that He was there for me when I had convinced myself that I was all alone. I might not have friends or family around me all day long, but I have God and with Him, I am never alone.

I want you to know that you are not alone. While we might not be together in the physical form, you have me in the palm of your hand, or on your digital device. I will be with you for as long as you need me. You can put me down whenever you want, or you can return to a specific section whenever you want to revisit something. Together we are going to learn more about ourselves and our capabilities.

Confidence Boosters

Before we move on to the next chapter, let us stop and take a look at some ways in which we can gain back some confidence we have lost along the way. It is normal to find yourself in a slump. I have found that, even when people say they are happy and that nothing phases them, they are masters at hiding their emotions. I do believe that everyone suffers a blow to their confidence during their lifetime. It is not a sign of weakness, and should not be viewed as such.

Comfort Zone

You need to find your anchor. A place where you feel safe and secure. A place where no one can rock your boat. Your comfort zone can be going for a hike in the mountains, watching your favorite movie, dancing to your favorite song, ordering a meal from your favorite restaurant, or writing in a journal. Your comfort zone is your bubble where you can go to gather your thoughts or forget that you have responsibilities for an hour or two.

Smile

We have established that your smile has the ability to light up the space around you. I know how difficult it is to plaster a smile on your face when your soul is just not feeling all that happy. If you are going through a loss or a disappointment, you might feel that there is nothing to smile or feel happy about. I am here to tell you to open your front door, take a step outside, and look at your surroundings. Whether you live in the concrete jungle, surrounded by high-rise buildings and speeding cars, or in a quiet neighborhood, where you can hear the flowers talking to each other, you will have something to smile about. The more you smile, the more you will believe that you are important and your confidence levels will rise.

One Step at a Time

Whether you had a traumatic experience or a setback at work, your confidence has been taken down a couple of notches. Self-doubt settles in and you do not feel that you are worthy. Take small steps to get yourself to where you were. One step at a time will help you build up your confidence again. Take everything in your stride. The pain and disappointment you experienced will still be there, but it is how you deal with the situation that makes the difference. Acknowledge what has happened and learn from it. Before you know it, you will be more confident than you were.

Nobody Is Perfect

As much as people like to believe they are perfect, that is just unrealistic. Perfection is something that has no flaws, such as scratches or cracks. As human beings, we would love to claim that we are perfect, and many do, but the truth is, we all have flaws. Our perfect imperfections are what make us unique. You should not make yourself out to be something you are not. You need to be comfortable in your own skin.

Socializing

This is a difficult one, but it is a necessary one. It is all good and well to hide behind one of the digital screens where we are protected from being judged, ridiculed, and made to feel worthless. We tend to view our screens as being our protections against the big bad world. It is time to toughen up, give the screens a break, and head outside. Whether you go to the store, to Church, the park, or a coffee shop, you are building your confidence. If you do not want to socialize with your friends or family, chat with strangers you cross paths with. You will find it easier to have a casual conversation with some random person, and it will fill you with confidence. Who knows you might learn something from the random person or the person might learn from you? Be brave.

Rebuilding Lost Confidence

Your confidence was obliterated, and you are afraid to do anything for fear of being hurt again. Having the confidence knocked out of you is not something anyone would wish on their worst enemy. You pour your heart and soul into everything you do, only to have someone come along and kick the air out of you. You are afraid to pick yourself up and move on after your bashing, but it is essential that you stand up, dust yourself off, and start over. Boosting your confidence is not to be confused with rebuilding your confidence, but you can use them in conjunction with each other to rebuild the faith you have in yourself.

Acknowledge the Situation

It is easy to shy away from a situation that breaks your confidence. You feel hurt, embarrassed, and angry because of something that happened that you had no control over. Yes, someone intentionally said or did something to negatively affect you. The best way to reverse the situation is to acknowledge what happened. No one is going to tell you that you have to confront the person or the situation, but you need to acknowledge what happened. This will start the healing process and build up your confidence. Once you acknowledge the trigger situation and accept what has happened, you are on the right path to regain your confidence and come back stronger than before.

Goals

This is one of my favorite pieces of advice to boost confidence. You need to have goals. Everyone needs to have goals. Something that you can look at when you feel like you are in a rut. Get yourself a journal or a notebook, and carry it around with you. At the start of each week, make a list of goals that you wish to achieve. It can be anything that resonates with you, whether it is reading a book, drinking more water, going for a walk, spring cleaning your home, or baking cookies and taking it to a care home in your community. You will feel good about yourself. Not only will it boost your confidence, but you will also be proving your importance to yourself and those around you.

Boosting Your Confidence Will Take Time

You might not see changes overnight, but the more consistent you are in building your confidence the more you will experience the changes in yourself. Take each day as it comes. Each person has a different experience that chiseled away their confidence. Some people are broken down in one day, others over a period of weeks, months, or years. You get to set the pace for your comeback. You will experience hurdles along the way but work through them with the tools you have been given. You will get there again. Have faith in yourself and trust in yourself.

Chapter 2:

Understanding Belief

You are most probably wondering how you can believe in something or someone if you are struggling with your confidence or self-importance. What good is believing when everything around you feels as though it is imploding? If you want a new car, you are told to believe and you will be rewarded. You are unhappy in your current job, and you are told to believe that something better will come along. How long should you believe in something before it happens?

It is so easy to say you should believe but you do not understand what or who you should believe in. As a child growing up, you had many beliefs. What happens when you reach the age of understanding the difference between fantasy and reality? Many of us believed in the Easter Bunny, the Tooth Fairy, and Santa Claus until we were either told the truth or figured it out for ourselves.

This chapter is going to be the stepping stones for the rest of this book. Together we are going to understand what belief is, why belief is important to who we are, what people believe in, and what you should believe in. This book is not going to force you into believing in something you are not ready to believe in. I have my beliefs which I am going to share with you.

As I have mentioned in the introduction, I too struggled to believe. I was angry at the world, my circumstances, God, and myself. Until I realized who I was and my importance to society, I was not ready to break the shackles that held my heart hostage. I needed to understand why having belief was important to finding myself. It is a process I had to work through, and it is a process everyone needs to go through.

What Is Belief?

According to the Merriam-Webster Dictionary, there are a couple of definitions of what belief means. Belief could be an instinct that we have that someone or something truly exists or is true; a gut feeling that what we are doing is good, right, or adds value to what we are doing; or that we trust in the abilities of someone. All these definitions lead us to the same conclusion, and that is putting our trust in someone or something that is greater than what we are such as religion, politicians, medicine, or science.

For our journey together, we are going to explore faith-based beliefs. We will leave the political-based beliefs to the politicians, the medical-based beliefs to the doctors, and the science-based beliefs to the scientists. Religion is a personal choice and a personal journey each person has to discover for themselves. I can share my experiences and the experiences of people I have spoken to. You can compare the examples as we move through the book, but at the end of the day, the choice you make is solely up to you.

Belief Systems

Having looked at the definitions, we have a better understanding of what beliefs are and how we, as humans, view them. Every human has a belief system. We can believe in whatever we want, and we use these belief systems to help us understand or have hope in what is going on around us. Human beings are curious by nature. If we find something that we want to believe in, we either observe what is going on, explore all the information before us, or ask questions. Basically, we want to make sense of what we may want to believe in.

We use these belief systems to help us cope with whatever situations we find ourselves in at a time when we are most vulnerable. Having belief, or believing, helps us cope with difficult situations. We can say that having belief in something is like having a security blanket that will soothe us in difficult times. Having a belief system in place is a coping mechanism that will ease our anxieties, fears, or lack of confidence. If we do not have a coping mechanism in place, we will be lost and wander around aimlessly. We will doubt everything we do; we will lose our confidence, and as such, we will be vulnerable and not be able to cling to anything we once thought was real.

What Do People Believe In?

We have to realize that we live in a world with over seven billion people. It is impossible that all seven billion people will have the same beliefs. "What do people believe in?" This is a question that does not have a right or wrong answer. Everyone has something they believe in, something that helps them cope with whatever is going on in their lives. Not everyone will have the same beliefs, and that is perfectly okay. As long as whoever you are asking the question to gives you their answers, that is their choice. We are not going to judge people based on their beliefs because it is their personal choice. I reached out to a couple of people who told me what they believe in.

I believe in fairies and unicorns. – Jessica, 4

I like to believe that everyone is good and that circumstances have made them do bad things. – Holly, 18

I believe that when I see doves congregating on my wall outside, looking in at me through the window, that God has sent my family to let me know that I am not alone. – Lynne, 47

I believe that one day, hopefully in the not too distant future, I will win the national lottery. – James, 39

I believe that every person living on this planet deserves to be free of ridicule. No one should be bullied because they do not conform to the way society expects them to be. – Jason, 18

I am a very positive person who sees the good in everything that happens around me. I like to believe that everything that happens, happens for a reason and even though we do not know why it is happening. God knows and He will reveal His plan when the time is right. — Aggie, 27

I believe in love at first sight. — Jon, 43

I believe that my Mummy will buy me a guinea pig when I turn 10. — Jenna, 8

I believe that God sent his only Son to die on the cross so that I could be free of sin. — Amanda, 29

I believe that when I pray, God will hear my prayers and answer me. It might not be when I want the answer, but rather when God feels that the time is right, which might be today, tomorrow, next week, in a couple of months, or next year. I do believe that God hears all prayers and is teaching us the real meaning of patience. — Micah, 57

I believe in aliens. When I say aliens, I mean people who think that they own the ground they walk on and expect everyone to jump through hoops to entertain their ideology that they are superior to all others, including God. — Jeremy, 21

As you can see, whether children believe in unicorns and fairies, winning the lottery, or God, everyone believes in something that means something special to them. As long as everyone believes in something that is meaningful to them, who are we to tell them that their beliefs are "dumb," "far-fetched," or "outrageous?"

Why Does It Matter What You Believe?

Everyone believes in something. Your beliefs might differ from the next person and you might not agree with them, but everyone has their own choices. When you believe in something with every fiber of your being, you hold onto that belief. Your belief is your foundation, and until proven otherwise, you will continue believing. When you live your life based on your beliefs, you are influencing the lives of people you come in contact with. People are quick to scrutinize how you portray yourself, and you will be put under their microscope as they wait for you to falter.

Nobody is perfect. Believe it or not, we are human and we do make wrong choices. Sometimes we do not realize that the choice we make will not have the desired outcome. When we know that we are doing something that goes against our belief, we are faced with a choice of continuing along the path we were on, or we stop to reassess and take a different path. It is not a sign of weakness to test your belief, it is a way to put your belief to the test.

What you believe in is important to you. It gives you hope and courage. Having belief strengthens your position as a person. It is no secret that we are living in trying times. The world is in crisis due to a global pandemic that is causing death and destruction each and every day. There is no cure as of yet. Yes, there are vaccinations that aim to prevent the virus from spreading, but there are many naysayers who have personally and publicly expressed their opinions regarding the vaccines. Personally, I believe that a cure will be found that will stop this virus in its tracks. I also believe that God will put an end to this virus. It is my belief and I will cling to it because it gives me strength and reassurance.

Does it matter what you believe in? If it is meaningful to you, then yes, it does matter. Speak about your beliefs, share your thoughts, and do not allow naysayers to convince you otherwise. When your beliefs become a reality, you will have the self-satisfaction of knowing that your faith and beliefs are a testimony to your journey through life.

"Indifference is the acid of life. It erodes all the spirit that's in us and makes us useless to anyone else. We have to stand for something, or our souls cease to breathe."

– Joan D. Chittister

What Should You Believe in?

Again, there are no right or wrong answers to this question. We will take a look at what people could believe in but each person has a personal choice. When trying to define what you should believe in, you will be influenced by the opinions of family, friends, and society but because you are your own person, with a mind of your own, no one can or should force you to believe in something you do not want to. If you are going to believe in something because you are told to, you are allowing others to take away your freedom of choice.

Your personal beliefs and values make you a unique human being. The person you are is defined by your uniqueness. You touch the lives of people around you because you choose to have faith and belief. Your optimism does not go unnoticed because you are unique. If you were doubting your importance when you started reading this book, I am choosing to believe that you are seeing yourself in a new light now.

Now that we have established your uniqueness and importance due to your beliefs, let us take a look at some points to fine-tune your beliefs. You can implement these points to strengthen your beliefs.

Believe in Yourself

This point cannot be stressed enough. You should always believe in yourself. Even if friends, family, or acquaintances tell you that you are wrong for believing in something, do not doubt yourself. If you believe you can climb a mountain, you will climb that mountain because that is what you believe. Challenge yourself to try something you have never tried before because you were afraid. Your belief in yourself will conquer fears.

Believe in Others

It is so easy to judge a book by its cover, and this is something we are all guilty of. We tend to judge people by their appearance, how they act, or what they say. As much as you do not want people to make assumptions about you, you should not make assumptions about others. If you have had a bad experience in the past, you should not base your opinion of others on that experience. Believe that all people are good and have good intentions. If you show fear or mistrust, they will see how you feel in your actions, and by the look on your face and in your eyes.

Believe That You Will Conquer Obstacles

In life, you will face many obstacles that will test your trust, faith, and beliefs. You will feel as if everything in your life is going wrong. Facing difficulties will fill you with doubt. How you deal with the issues will make you stronger. Remember, no one can steal your happiness and self-worth unless you give up. It is important to keep believing and know that there is a light at the end of the tunnel. Personally, I believe that God doesn't give us obstacles we cannot overcome.

Hope

Having hope strengthens belief. If you believe in something, you have hope that your belief will come to fruition. For instance, if you have lost your job due to cutbacks in the company, you hope with everything in you that you will find another job. You believe you will find a job, and when you add hope, you are strengthening your belief. Without hope, you will feel a void, and self-doubt will start eating at your belief.

Believe in Forgiveness

Imagine being in a situation where someone close to you has spread vicious lies to your relatives. As a result, your family members cut you out of their lives. The instigator has accomplished what they set out to do and carries on as if nothing is wrong. Years later, when that person is fragile and broken, you forgive them for breaking your family apart. You feel lighter as you no longer have that intense anger. You reach out to your lost family members and start mending the broken fences.

This is a tough one for everyone. It is easier to hold a grudge against someone who hurt you than to move past it. We have all been there but it is healing to the soul to forgive. We all say and do stuff in the heat of an argument. You cannot take back the hurtful words or actions, but forgiveness will set you free.

Ready. Set. Go!

Now that you have an understanding of what belief is, you are ready to embark on the next part of your life journey. You know that everyone believes in something. We touched on a couple of points of what you should be believing in, but there are many more. Do not underestimate your beliefs. You are stronger than you give yourself credit for, you are courageous, you are kind, and your soul is beautiful. Whenever you feel doubt creeping in and threatening your beliefs, arm yourself with positive affirmations. Stand in front of the mirror and tell yourself that you are the best person you know. Say it until you believe it.

Chapter 3:

Analyzing Beliefs

"Your beliefs become your thoughts,

Your thoughts become your words,

Your words become your actions,

Your actions become your habits,

Your habits become your values,

Your values become your destiny."

–Mahatma Gandhi

Whether you have been struggling with your beliefs or if you want confirmation about the path you are on, you are where you need to be. We have covered the basics of your importance and belief, and we understand who and what we are. We are learning about what our purpose in life is, and what we can do to improve or strengthen what we believe.

I previously mentioned that what you believe in, is a personal choice. If a toddler wants to believe in the Tooth Fairy, that is their choice. As they get older, they will realize that what they believed is no longer relevant to their lives. If you want to base your beliefs on something that makes you feel important to yourself, believe away. You are under no obligation to share your beliefs with anyone.

This chapter is going to be about analyzing your beliefs. We are going to explore the good, the bad, and the ugly beliefs you have in yourself. This is going to change the way you think about yourself. There is so much negativity surrounding us that it ends up latching onto us, and without realizing it, we spread negativity in the way we talk to people or by our actions. Together we are going to build up your confidence, show you that you are important, and spread positivity.

Core Beliefs

We have established that our beliefs are important to us. Unfortunately, our beliefs include what we believe and think about ourselves, other people, the future, and the world. These deep impressions that are ingrained in us are called core beliefs. Without realizing it, these core beliefs affect our interpretations of how we perceive what is good or bad, right or wrong, and positive or negative. What we believe in has the ability to affect our behaviors and actions both positively and negatively.

Our core beliefs are often misguided in the sense that, when we believe in something, we do not want to see or hear what anyone else has to say. No one is going to tell you it is wrong to believe in something. However, it is good to analyze your beliefs to remain relevant to the present day or circumstances. All too often we go through life holding onto beliefs that we have had since we were children, something our parents enforced upon us or something our grade school teachers taught us. As adults, we carry a lot of memories from our childhood. These memories include things we believed because it was told to us on many occasions. Without realizing it, we will be doing something and the memory pops up and we find ourselves questioning whether we should be doing this or that because as a child, it was wrong.

I spoke to someone who shared a childhood memory of something they believed in:

I remember my parents telling me that I could not swim for at least an hour after I had eaten something because I would drown. I believed them because I trust their judgment. I carried this belief with me when I went to work as an au pair in another country. The children had just finished eating their turkey subs, they were huge portions, and then jumped into the pool. I panicked and tried to get them out, telling them they had to wait for the food to settle. Their father, who was a doctor, told me that it was okay for the children to swim and that there was no proof that you could not swim after eating a meal.

Let us analyze our core beliefs and learn to unpack what we have learned until now. I would like to leave a gentle reminder that I am not, under any circumstances, trying to change or alter what you believe in. I have stated that this book is not about judgment or bullying. I would like you to have an open mind as we work through this section. I promise that I am not going to brainwash you into believing what I have to say. I am presenting you with the research I have done, as well as personal stories from people I have spoken to while doing my research.

Where Do Beliefs Come From?

Everyone needs something to believe in, whether it was something we learned at school, at home, at church, in the store, or in the media. When analyzing our beliefs, we need to look a little deeper and look at various sources that influence us. Beliefs should be challenged to ensure that you are equipped with the facts and knowledge of what you believe is right for your thought process. Many of us accept beliefs because we trust the person or persons who "made us see the light." Let us have a look at some of the sources that we should be basing our beliefs on.

Evidence

What will you do if you are approached by someone telling you to join up with some or other program where you are guaranteed to triple your $50 investment in a year? They will go into detail and convince you why you should join up. The details they are providing you with, whether it be statistics, figures, or proof of their payouts sounds like an answer to your financial woes. Would you sign up without researching for yourself? No, you will ask questions, you will search for information on Google, you will read articles, or you will read reviews about the company before making a decision.

This is what you should be doing when it comes to beliefs. Investigate your belief. Read articles. Search for the information you need to know about your belief. If you want to share your belief with others, show them the proof so that they know that your belief is justified.

Tradition

Some beliefs are passed down by families and society. As free-thinking people, you do have a choice to believe in these traditions. You might be facing ridicule for your choices, but you will need to decide for yourself, without pressure from those around you or society.

Examples of tradition-based beliefs include:

- Following in the footsteps of generations of family members before you. If you come from a family with a history in the medical profession, it will be up to you to keep that tradition alive by entering into the medical field in some or other capacity.

- If your family is part of a certain religious denomination, you are expected to remain a member of that religion. You might not agree with the principles of the church. You might have many reasons for not wanting to be part of the church or no church. It is your duty and the expectation from your family to continue with the family tradition.

- Politics is a tricky tradition for many families and societies. If your family line has been supporting one political party since before your existence, you are expected to keep the momentum by believing in that party.

Challenge your beliefs. If you are not happy with carrying on a tradition, you should have the freedom to make a choice without being pressured. The world has evolved, and it continues to evolve every day. Be the change you want for yourself.

Authority

We have touched on authority previously, where family or teachers teach us what they believe. As an adult, you have the freedom to challenge your family and teachers by searching for evidence to test their beliefs. If the beliefs you grew up believing do not meet your expectations, you can adjust them to suit you based on your evidence.

Association by Influence

Everyone has a friend or a group of friends that have opinions and beliefs that rub off onto us. You never realize that their beliefs influence you until a situation presents itself where that belief rears its head. There is nothing wrong with adopting the beliefs of your friends. You do need to establish whether their beliefs are what you want for yourself or whether you were forced. Remember, you are your own person and not a pack animal that operates on the opinions of others.

Belief by Revelation

Everyone has a sixth sense or intuition that cannot be explained. These beliefs are meaningful to us. If you believe in signs, such as the feather, put it to the test. Challenge these signs as you would any of the other sources of belief. Trust your intuition to guide you.

In 2013, my mom passed away suddenly. I was heartbroken, lost, and alone. My daily routine consisted of working up to 20 hours a day, seven days a week to keep me from thinking. This routine went on for five months. One day, while I was working on my laptop, I noticed something floating down from the ceiling. There was not a breath of wind and no movement in the air. It was a little feather. As I watched the feather making its way down, I was paralyzed. The feather continued its downward fall, gently navigating its way over to where I was working. It came to land on my keyboard. I stared at the feather and suddenly burst into tears as a sense of calmness washed over me. I believed it was a sign from my mom, that I need to stop mourning her and a reminder that she will always be with me. Now, whenever I see a feather, I believe that my mom has popped in for a visit. – Melissa, 48

The Nitty Gritty Side of Core Beliefs

A secret door was exposed when you explored some, or all, of your core beliefs. You know that your beliefs had to start somewhere, but you never gave it much thought until now, when you started challenging your beliefs. You are digging deeper by analyzing what you believe in. You have questions, and the only way to find the answers you desire is to scratch around and open all the secret doors in your mind.

While we poke around through the cobwebs in the secret rooms, keep your notebook or journal handy. As memories start washing over you, write them down. Write down anything you may remember such as smells, emotions, and words uttered. Some of your beliefs may be brand new, and some may be so old that they are stuck in the archives, covered in thick layers of mind dust. Spring cleaning is called for every now and again to evaluate, format, and upgrade—in other words, make your beliefs more relevant to where you are in your life's journey.

Our core beliefs consist of two main components: positive and negative. All it takes is for one person to say something positive or negative for the seeds to germinate and grow. What you are told will be either life-affirming, or soul-crushing. As mentioned previously, you can, and should, challenge your core beliefs. Do not allow the opinions of others to dictate or influence you. You are your own person, not to be compared with a sibling, a friend, or an employee.

Negative Beliefs

Everyone has a speck of negativity inside. These negative beliefs follow us around as if to coerce us to walk the path that will make us believe the negativity. Your beliefs are limited because you are choosing to believe in something you have not challenged. Do not allow the negative beliefs to cloud your judgment of yourself, the space around you, the truth, or the people you come in contact with.

Some examples of negative beliefs that you believe to be true:

- I am worthless and I will never amount to anything.

- I am an idiot. I am forever doing things wrong and putting the sugar in the fridge is an example of my idiocy.

- Intruders are hiding behind the boundary walls. They are waiting for me to turn off my lights before they break in. I will stay awake tonight to protect my home.

- Veronica is a terrible influence on the people around her. I do not trust her one bit, she has ulterior motives.

Positive Beliefs

Personally, I do believe that being positive is something I can control. I do realize that not everyone will agree with my beliefs, and that is perfectly fine with me. I have the freedom to choose, as do you, whatever I want. You should not have to be afraid to be positive or express your optimism. If others do not agree with you, it is their choice but you are enabling your beliefs and you know, you can achieve anything you set your mind to.

Some examples of positive beliefs. You could turn positive beliefs into affirmations to help keep you on the right track:

- I am destined to accomplish something amazing. Time will tell, but until then, I will keep believing.

- I am gorgeous. My body, wrinkles, and blemishes might not agree, but when I look in the mirror, I see perfection.

Are Beliefs Worth Changing?

We have spent time unpacking and analyzing our beliefs. Some of the beliefs we have held onto since before we could remember. A lot of those beliefs were forced or imprinted on us when we were children, and as we grew up, we clung to them. Without realizing it, a lot of what you believe in is clouding your judgment of how you view the world around you. No matter how you came to believe in something, you should challenge it to see if it falls within your personal beliefs.

Having a belief or many beliefs is personal to you. You know how you feel when you believe in something. You are passionate and filled with excitement about something you have discovered, whether it is a new television series, a new cookie flavor, or a new blend of coffee. You are desperate for everyone around you to try out your discoveries. Not everyone is going to share your excitement because everyone has their own opinions.

You cannot force people into believing something they do not want to. As human beings, we have the right to make our own choices even if they are not what we would have chosen, and that is okay. You do not want to take away someone's freedom of choice, because then you are doing what you do not want people to do to you. Being labeled as a bully is not a good label to have, as it will follow you wherever you go. Be mindful of those around you, and their choices.

Eliminate negative thinking, and surround yourself with positive. Use your notebook or journal and make a list of five positive actions or things that you believe you need to work on. Focus on the positive list for a week, and build on it. Your list could look something like this:

- This week, I am going to wake up half an hour earlier each morning and go for a 15-minute walk around the neighborhood.

- This week I am not going to allow Tracey to bully me. It is time to show her, and all the other Tracey's, that I have got feelings and that they are not going to get me down anymore.

- This week, I am going to cut refined sugar out of my diet. It is going to be difficult, but I do believe I can do it.

- I want to perform a couple of random acts of kindness this week, whether it is buying some groceries, a hot meal, or a toy for someone who needs to be reminded that there are good people out there.

Making a list will help you with your self-worth, as well as boost your confidence. It is good to have goals, and I believe everyone should have multiple lists around their homes that remind them who they are, what they want to accomplish, and the obstacles that were overcome.

Should Beliefs Be Changed?

In answer to the original question asked about whether beliefs are worth changing, the answer would be that it falls into the personal choice category. If, after having analyzed your beliefs, you feel that there is room for improvement or fine-tuning, tinker away. If you do not believe that your belief bank needs an update, then you do nothing other than keeping an open mind and re-evaluate your core beliefs every so often.

It cannot be stressed enough that, whenever you are in doubt or faced with a situation that you feel needs to be reassessed, challenge your beliefs. If you decide to challenge your beliefs, and subsequently change what you believed in, that is up to you. If you need some help deciding whether you should analyze your beliefs—hello and welcome to the help center. Okay, not funny, but a giggle here and there is definitely a good tonic for the soul—at least, that is what my grandma used to tell me!

Use the tools you have been given to help you with your assessment and see where your beliefs will lead you to. Challenge the origins of your beliefs by looking at the evidence, traditions, authority, influence, and revelation. Do not forget to take your positive and negative beliefs along. Categorize your beliefs into four sections namely yourself, those around you, your surroundings, and the future. Again, use the journal to help you make points. Change because you want to, not because you need to fit in with various stereotypes.

Upgrading Beliefs

You have analyzed the beliefs that you have stored away in your belief bank. Many of those beliefs are buried under thick layers of add-on beliefs you have gathered throughout the weeks, months, and years. You have learned that beliefs cloud your perception between fact or fiction. After years of believing everything that was said about you, the scales have fallen from your eyes and you are seeing clearly.

If, after analyzing your beliefs, you decide that you want to make changes that will reflect positively. You are eager to unpack all your beliefs in one sitting and start fresh but it is not as simple as it sounds. It is not as if you have emptied your closet, donated all your clothing to Goodwill, went off to Target, and bought new clothes because you did not like the color scheme or the style.

Change can be overwhelming, especially when it comes to digging into your mind palace and scratching around the dust bunnies to find what you want. Will the process of changing beliefs be easy? Probably not. Beliefs are most often connected to memories, and prodding around the memories could have one of three outcomes depending on your experience. You could experience anger, sadness, or be neutral to whatever you are going through. No one can tell you how you should be feeling or how you should be coping with the new realities of your beliefs as you embark on the journey of self-discovery.

Stepping Stones: Helpful Tips to Changing Beliefs

Changes will not happen in the blink of an eye. It can take days, weeks, months, or years to break the habit of a certain belief. As you move through the process of altering your beliefs, do not be afraid to challenge yourself. Keep your journal handy so that you can make notes and plot your plan of action.

- Know what your core belief is, and challenge it in terms of where and how it affects your life.

- Look at the research you found while trying to understand your beliefs.

- Weigh up the pros and cons of the belief you have been holding onto since you were a child. Look at the good and the bad, and decide the path forward.

- Thinking about the beliefs you had before you started doubting yourself, recall your attitude or behavior towards people or specific situations.

- Put yourself to the test by questioning the belief you are challenging and where it will feature in your life.

- Eradicate a belief that has been proven to be redundant. Adopt a new belief or strengthen a belief that needs a little more affirmation.

- Have daily goals. List your goals. Read your goal lists every day and keep striving to reach those goals.

"Belief overflows to behavior. First we need to change what we believe. When we truly change what we believe, we'll gladly change how we behave."

— Craig Groeschel

Chapter 4:

Understanding Religion: Different

Religions

The topic of religion is very private, and not one that should be forced on everyone. Many people skirt around the topic of religion for fear of offending those who do not share the same views, who are not on the same journey, or being ridiculed for speaking out. We live in a world that has many different religions and each religion has multiple denominations. It is understandable why people have a problem choosing a religion when there are so many different opinions being forced on people.

Personally, I do not go out onto the street and choose a random stranger to share my views with. For all I know, and with my luck, I would probably put my foot in my mouth. In all seriousness, religion is not one-size-fits-all. Religion is a personal choice decision that cannot, and should not, be forced on people. If you want someone to believe in any religion, you have to let them decide. The more you force your views and beliefs on people, the more you are pushing them to explore other avenues.

If you want someone to join you on your religious journey, you have to give them the time and space to figure things out for themselves. You can plant the seeds. You can give them food for thought. You can let people see how you treat people in less fortunate situations. In short, your actions will speak louder than any words when you allow them to observe you doing God's work.

I spoke to Roxy and she told me about her time as a youth leader. She told me how the church where she was a volunteer youth leader would offer courses for teenagers. The teenagers came from broken and dysfunctional homes where the parents had all but given up hope of having normal, healthy teenagers. According to Roxy, the teenagers were experimenting with drugs, drinking alcohol, smoking weed, and having sex—these children ranged from ages 13 to 15. During the camp weekends, the children were introduced to the Holy Spirit. Roxy remembers that many of the children were not ready to meet Jesus Christ, much less be filled with the Holy Spirit, as they would leave the session and head off to the furthest corner of the camping area to light up a cigarette or a joint.

Jumping into the future, Roxy remained in contact with most of the teenagers she met during her youth leader days. Among the 30-odd teenagers that went on the camps, there are maybe 12 that have turned their lives around and are following the gospel. Others have strayed, either still doing drugs, drinking heavily, been divorced and married, cheating on spouses, and one has committed suicide.

What Is Religion?

We go through life assuming we know everything about certain topics until someone challenges our knowledge. It is then that we realize that what we know is information based on what we were taught by our peers. When it comes to religion, many people fade into the background for fear of offending someone. It seems as if Christians are placed under a microscope and everyone keeps a very close eye on them. Personally, this is something I have been part of, as well as participated in.

The following passage tells us that we should not be criticising or pointing out flaws in other people without taking a good look at ourselves.

Judge not, that you be not judged. For with what judgment you judge, you will be judged; and with the measure you use, it will be measured back to you. And why do you look at the speck in your brother's eye, but do not consider the plank in your own eye? Or how can you say to your brother, 'Let me remove the speck from your eye'; and look, a plank is in your own eye? Hypocrite! First remove the plank from your own eye, and then you will see clearly to remove the speck from your brother's eye (*New King James Bible*, 1982, Matt. 7:1-5).

After reading this passage, you realize that you are judging people because of what they do. The time has come to stop looking at others and looking for their faults. Clean your own home before you attempt to clean your neighbor's home.

Definition of Religion

According to the Merriam-Webster Dictionary, the definition of religion is believing in God, or a group of deities. It is also a structured system of beliefs, organized rules to worship deities or ceremonies where individuals practice their devotion to God.

My definition of religion is that I believe in the trinity; the Father, the Son, and the Holy Spirit. I believe that when I pray, I pray to the Father, through the Son, in the Spirit. I also believe Jesus Christ died on the cross so that my past, present, and future sins would be forgiven. This does not mean that I should sin more because I am forgiven, it means that I do not have to pray for forgiveness each time I do something I should not be doing. Something each believing person should remember is: "For He made Him who knew no sin to be sin for us, that we might become the righteousness of God in Him," (*New King James Bible*, 1982, Cor. 5:21).

Depending on where you are in your faith and belief system, your interpretation of religion will differ to fit in with what you have learned from school, family, religious leaders, or independent research.

Exploring Different Religions

We live in a world that has a population of over seven billion inhabitants. These seven billion people are split up and dispersed across seven different continents across the world. The continents are Australia, Europe, South, and North America, Africa, Antarctica, and Asia. Each of these seven continents has countries, provinces, counties, towns, villages, and so forth. When considering the number of inhabitants there are in the world, inquiring minds want to understand how others view religion, traditions, cultures, and beliefs.

There are hundreds of different religions in this beautifully diverse world of ours. Many might not agree with the principles of other religions, but it is not up to us to force people into agreeing with us. We should not be judging a person based on their chosen religion. If you happen to find out that your best friend follows a religion that you do not agree with, it does not mean that you should end your friendship. The chances are, if the person is your best friend, they will respect your religion and they will expect the same in return.

Religions are not to be confused with denominations. Each religion branches out to form its group under a religious umbrella. We will explore some of the religions and touch on some of the more well-known denominations as we learn about our faith-based beliefs. You want open and honest feedback, and that is what you will be getting. There will be no sugar coating or coercing you into changing your views of a specific religion or denomination. You have the freedom of choice to believe what you want.

Islam

In the year 570 A.D., in the Saudi Arabian town of Mecca, the prophet Muhammad was born. Members of the Islamic religion are referred to as Muslims, and they are believed to worship one God. God has different names in the various religions, but no matter what the names are, it all turns back to the all-knowing God. For the purpose of the Islamic religion, God in Arabic is Allah.

It is believed that the angel Gabriel visited the prophet Muhammad to spread and teach Allah's message to all mankind. Muslims live according to the word of Allah, and they believe that prophets are responsible for teaching the law according to Allah. They put all their hope, belief, trust, and faith in Allah. Muslims believe in the prophet Muhammad for his teachings, as Christians and Jews believe in the teachings from the word.

Place of Worship

Muslims practice praise and worship in mosques. While mosques are more commonly used as prayer locations, they are also used as homeless shelters, wedding ceremonies, funerals, religious occasions such as Ramadan, and religious instruction. The mosques are unique, as when they are built, they feature an ornamental artifact indicating the direction of Mecca. Friday prayers at the mosque are reserved for men, while women pray in different rooms. The most important shrines and mosques in the Islamic religion are the Al-Aqsa mosque in Jerusalem, Prophet Muhammad's mosque in Medina, and the Kaaba shrine in Mecca.

The Written Word

The Quran is as important to the Muslims, as the Bible is to the Christians. There are similarities between the Bible and the Quran such as the basic scriptures and revelations that were shown to the prophet Muhammad. Muslims believe that the Quran was documented by record keepers on behalf of Muhammad, who could not read or write. The Quran consists of 114 surahs or chapters which are believed to be teachings to Muhammad by the angel Gabriel.

Religious Principles and Beliefs

Every religion has a set of beliefs and principles that are important to its faith. These beliefs and principles strengthen the faith in their religion and ensure that all followers remain grounded. The Islamic religion has the "five pillars" which are important for Muslims to live by.

- Shahada is acknowledging your faith in Allah and believing in Muhammad.

- Salat is the commitment to praying at sunrise, midday, afternoon, sunset, and evenings—five times a day.

- Zakat is the commitment to helping people who need assistance regardless of gender, ethnicity, or religion.

- Sawm is a reminder to fast during the holy month of Ramadan. Fasts start at sunrise and end at sunset for 30 days, depending on the cycle of the moon.

- Hajj is the promise to join a pilgrimage to Mecca once during their lifetime.

Religious Holidays

The Muslim faith, much like any other religion, celebrates religious holidays as well as cultural observances. The Islamic calendar features the following holidays:

- Al-Hijra is known as the Islamic New Year. The significance of Al-Hijra is that it commemorates the prophet Muhammad's journey from Mecca to Medina coming to an end.

- Eid ul-Adha is known as the "festival of sacrifice." This holiday spans over four days representing the faithfulness and obedience which Abraham showed to God by his willingness to sacrifice his son, Isaac. Eid ul-Adha is a celebratory event that marks the end of the yearly pilgrimage to Mecca.

- Eid ul-Fitr marks the end of a 30-day fast where all Muslims fast from sunrise to sunset. The 30-day fast is celebrated over three days. Celebrations are attended by family and friends to mark the end. During Eid ul-Fitr, all Muslims will go to early morning prayers at the mosque.

- The Prophet's Birthday is a special day where members of the Muslim faith celebrate the birth of the prophet Muhammad.

- Ramadan is the start of the 30-day fast, according to the moon cycle. As previously mentioned, Muslims will observe 30 days of fasting from sunrise to sunset where they will refrain from eating or drinking during these times. The fast will come to an end with the celebration of Eid ul-Fitr.

Religious Denominations

Examples of various Islamic denominations within the Muslim faith are:

- Nation of Islam
- Alawite
- Wahhabi
- Shiites
- Sunni (History.com Editors, 2018)

Judaism

The Judaism religion has been practiced by Jews for over 4,000 years. Jews believe in one true God who speaks to followers through prophets. Jews believe that God rewards believers who do good and are faithful and punish those who commit sins. Where Christians believe that Jesus is the Messiah, Jews do not follow this belief. It is believed the Jews believe the Messiah is still to come one day.

Place of Worship

When King David ruled the Israeli nation in 1000 B.C., the first temple was constructed by Solomon in Jerusalem. The temple was destroyed by the Babylonians in 587 B.C. and the Jews went into hiding. A second temple was built but was destroyed by the Romans in 70 A.D. After the destruction of the second temple, Jews no longer had a place to worship as a group. The destruction led followers of the Jewish faith to construct synagogues where they could practice praise and worship. Members of the Jewish faith continue to practice their religion in synagogues throughout the world.

The Written Word

Where the Muslims have the Quran, Jews have the Tanakh, which is known as the Hebrew Bible. The Tanakh features the books of the Old Testament that are found in the Christian Bible. As the Jews do not acknowledge Jesus as being the Messiah, the New Testament is excluded from the Tanakh. Although the Old Testament features in the Tanakh, the books are not in the same order. In fact, the first five books of the Tanakh are known as the Torah, or the Pentateuch. The purpose of the Torah occupying the first five books of the Tanakh is the guidelines of the laws the Jewish faith are meant to follow.

Religious Principles and Beliefs

We all know the story about the creation of the earth as depicted in Genesis. God created the earth in six days and declared the seventh day as a day of rest. In the Jewish culture, the seventh day is known as Shabbat. Jews observe Shabbat by spending time in prayer beginning at sunset on Fridays until sunset on Saturdays. Shabbat is considered a time where there are no external distractions such as work, worldly possessions such as electrical devices, or driving. The time is spent with family in worship at home or synagogues.

Religious Holidays

As one of the oldest religions, I believe that Judaism has the most important religious holidays out of all the religions. These religious holidays have been practiced since the beginning of time, and all holidays or celebrations that are practiced in the present time have branched off of and evolved due to the Jewish traditions.

- Passover is an ancient tradition on the Jewish calendar which celebrates the freedom of enslaved Jews in Egypt. Passover spans over seven to eight days and is based on the biblical story of when Egypt was cursed with plagues. Moses, a Hebrew prophet, was led by God to free the Jews from oppression and slavery during the reign of his brother, Rameses. One of the plagues that swept through Egypt was that of the death of first-born sons. God saved the Jewish children by passing over their homes.

- Rosh Hashanah is commonly known as the Jewish New Year. It is a day of celebration for the birth of the universe and humankind.

- Yom Kippur or Day of Atonement is one of the holiest religious holidays on the Jewish calendar. According to the Jewish belief, Yom Kippur is when God decides what is going to happen to Jews. During this time of fasting and praying, Jews are told to pray for forgiveness for any sins they may have committed.

- Hanukkah, or the Festival of Lights, is a celebration where members of the Jewish faith pray, give and receive gifts, and light the menorah for eight days.

Religious Denominations

Examples of various Judaism denominations within the Jewish faith include:
- Orthodox Judaism
- Reform Judaism
- Conservative Judaism
- Humanistic Judaism (History.com Editors, 2018)

Christianity

Christianity is believed to be the most followed religion with over two billion followers across the world. The first Christians are believed to have been Jews that converted after the death and resurrection of Jesus. The first church was created in Jerusalem and attended by the Jewish converts, as well as gentiles who wanted to be part of the Christian faith.

Regardless of what we believe today, early Christians believed that if it was not for the work done by the apostle Paul, Christianity would not be where it is today. Paul's story is one of awe and inspiration, as before he dedicated his life to Christ, he used to persecute Christians. Through divine intervention or a supernatural encounter with Jesus, Paul went on to build churches in Africa, Europe, and the Roman Empire. It is also widely speculated that Paul had a hand in writing 13 of the 27 books of the New Testament.

Place of Worship

When asking someone where they worship, many will say that they go to church. From a personal perspective, and from having discussions with Christians during my research, I came to the conclusion that churches are everywhere. The church building where people congregate to worship, praise, have weddings or funerals, or baptisms.

The following verse leads me to believe that this is what a church is: "For where two or three are gathered together in My name, I am there in the midst of them," (*New King James Bible*, 1982, Matt. 18:20).

This is a verse that came to me when the world went into lockdown due to a global pandemic. Gatherings were forbidden, and if we wanted to worship—regardless of religion, we had to find alternative options. If we were lucky enough to be living with people, we started home church or we joined our congregations via Zoom calls. There were those who searched YouTube or Facebook for online church services.

No one knows if, or when, the pandemic will fizzle out, but for the moment, while we are practicing social distancing and not participating in group events at churches, our new normal is social media or home church. Any way it is done is perfectly fine because it has been proven that you do not need a building to practice religion.

The Written Word

Christians have Bibles. There are no other names for the Bible as is noted in the Jewish or Muslim faith. The Christian Bible consists of 66 books which are divided into two sections.

The first half of the Bible consists of 39 books and documents the history of the Jews. The Old Testament goes into detail about the laws that all believers should be adhering to and it gives us an in-depth look at the descendants of the early prophets. There are also many prophecies about the birth of Jesus or the coming of the Messiah.

The second half of the Bible consists of 27 books and documents the teachings of Jesus Christ, the miracles He performed, His death, and resurrection. The Christian religion is based on what is written in the New Testament. The last book in the New Testament is a prophecy that predicts how the world will end at the time of the second coming when Jesus returns to walk among us on this earth.

Religious Principles and Beliefs

Christianity has many beliefs and principles to live by. If you open the Bible to any random page, you are guaranteed to read something that will speak directly to your heart. Let us take a look at some of the examples or a teaser if you might, of what you could look forward to when you read the Bible.

- As with the Judaism religion, Christians believe that there is only one God. We know that God created the earth in six days, and rested on the seventh day.

- Christianity is based on the life and death of Jesus Christ. Christians believe that Jesus died on the cross to redeem us of our sins and to save us from eternal condemnation. Jesus was resurrected after His death where He sits at the right-hand side of the throne, beside our Father God.

- The New Testament prepares Christians for the day that Jesus returns to the earth. The book of Revelations prophesied about the second coming. In modern times, people are speculating when the second coming will happen but the truth is, no one can say for sure. Yes, many will argue that the prophecies detailed in the book of Revelations indicate that the world will be ending soon, but again, we were not given the gift of foretelling and therefore we should not be making predictions. God will send Jesus back when the time is right.

- Christians believe in the Trinity which is God the Father, Jesus Christ, the Son, and the Holy Spirit. As mentioned previously, when you are praying, you pray in the Spirit, through the Son, to God, the Father.

- The symbol that represents Christianity is the cross.

In addition to the beliefs in the Christian faith, we can look at some of the main points of what Jesus teaches us throughout the New Testament.

- The number one takeaway from the New Testament is that we must love God.

- "This is the first and great commandment. And the second is like it: 'You shall love your neighbor as yourself.' On these two commandments hang all the Law and the Prophets," (*New King James Bible*, 1982, Matt. 22:38-40).

- Forgive people that have hurt you. You might not be able to forget what has happened, but forgiveness will release the anger and hatred that has you captive.

- Asking God for forgiveness for sins committed. This is a difficult one that is often misinterpreted. God does not expect us to go down a list of sins we have committed from the time we could think. Remember, God sacrificed His only Son so that we could have a clean slate. During your time of prayer, pray for forgiveness for any sins committed on the day. The past is gone, and in the name of Jesus Christ, you are a new creation. "For He made Him who knew no sin to be sin for us, that we might become the righteousness of God in Him," (*New King James Bible*, 1982, Cor. 5:21).

Religious Holidays

Christmas is not all about the gifts, and who gets the biggest and most expensive gifts nor is it about the all-you-can-eat feast. On the 25th of December, Christians around the world celebrate the birth of Jesus Christ.

Easter is not about the fluffy bunnies and mystical chickens leaving chocolate eggs all around your garden. Easter is all about the crucifixion of Jesus on the Friday, and His resurrection three days later, on the Sunday.

Ascension Day is celebrated by Christians 40 days after the resurrection of Jesus. On Ascension Day, Jesus leaves the earth to take His place at the right-hand side of the throne, beside God.

Religious Denominations

The Christian religion is divided into three sections namely Catholics, Orthodox, and Protestants. The Protestant branch is one of the most diverse, having hundreds, if not thousands, of denominations. There are many different Protestant denominations that differ from the traditional sense of Christianity in the way they interpret the Bible and understand the church.

Some of the denominations you may have heard of include:

- Baptist
- Methodist
- Anglican
- Presbyterian
- Episcopalian
- Assemblies of God
- Seventh-Day Adventist
- The Church of Jesus Christ of Latter-day Saints, also commonly known as Mormons
- Jehovah Witness (History.com Editors, 2018)

Other Religions

Islam, Judaism, and Christianity are three of the most practiced religions in the world. This does not mean that they are the only religions being practiced. The list is endless when it comes to religions and denominations. Not all religions believe that there is a God.

Other religious beliefs, or lack of, include:

- Buddhism
- Hinduism
- Sikhism
- New Age
- Occult
- Paganism

- Wicca

- Atheism

These religious beliefs, whether we agree or not, are widely held across the world. Many may not agree with the practice of certain religions but it is up to each individual who or what they believe in. You may not agree with certain religions and your first instinct would be to convince people to convert, you have to remember that it is their choice. Just as you do not want people to force you into changing what you believe in, you have to respect them. From your side, you can show people your faith and belief through your actions.

Chapter 5:

Understanding Religion: The Ups and Downs of Religion

Not everyone is on the same page when it comes to religion, much less being positive when there is so much going on in the world. Everyone has their theories about what is going on, but that is a whole lot of speculation fueled by self-appointed sofa conspiracy theorists. In a time when the world was dealt a devastating blow that continues to cause death and destruction, we saw an increase in self-educated sofa doctors, scientists, or professors. People turned to the search engines for their answers, and if they did not like the answers that the real professionals provided, they collaborated with those who gave simple, yet inaccurate, information. The social media platforms, from Facebook and Twitter to Instagram and YouTube, were buzzing with misinformation.

I have spoken to many people from all walks of life. There are people who have jumped on the misinformation bus and spread false information while riling people up with their version of what they believe to be the truth. There are people who thrive on causing tension amongst groups, whether it be political, race-related, gender-based, or anything that robs people of their freedom of choice, including the freedom of religion.

There are those who say that they believe in God and that their religion is important to them, only to do the opposite of their faith. Just when you think you are not alone in your faith, you witness those same people saying and doing things that go against your beliefs. You start questioning their actions and you find yourself questioning your faith. I am not implying that all people act in this manner, but I have personally witnessed people who do not practice what they preach.

The Pros and Cons of Religion

In my experience, everything in life has its ups and downs. Whether it is a lifestyle, health, occupation, relationships, and even religion, nothing is ever perfect. Whatever we are presented with, we have to accept the positives and negatives that come with it.

Religion is no different. Believers will defend their beliefs and hold true to what they believe to be the truth according to the word, and non-believers will challenge your beliefs. In this section, I will share why I believe in God and why my beliefs are important to me. I will also present you with the pros and cons of putting all your faith in someone you cannot physically see but that you know is there.

It's All About God

When people find out that I have chosen to dedicate my life to God, they want to know if it is worth putting all my faith in someone I cannot see or how can I trust that God is really with me. I cannot give a definitive answer other than I know in my gut that I am not alone. Before I gave my life to God and became a reborn Christian, I was an angry person. I felt as if I had no purpose. I was alone and confused, and I struggled to join social groups. I had no trust in people because I had been disappointed one too many times. In my opinion, people were quick to judge people based on the way they look, the way they dress, the color of their skin, and just their overall actions. I did not like the feelings I encountered. I knew that I wanted to be someone I could be proud of.

I chose to dedicate my life to God because I believed that He was there for me, even though I could not see Him. I do understand that everybody has different experiences and that what I experience cannot be compared to others. I can say for certain that, by acknowledging that God is a part of my life, I am genuinely happy with the path I am on. I am in no way implying that everything is sunshine and roses. I do experience difficult situations, ones where I feel as though the odds are against me and that I will never recover, but I always manage to overcome those odds.

One of the people I spoke to during my research told me that God never gives us obstacles we cannot work through and that it is a test of our faith. What God really wants from His children is to rely on Him in times of darkness.

The Cons of Believing in Religion

The cons of believing in religion are not necessarily based on believing in God, but more the literal interpretation of the Bible. There are many people who follow the Bible without looking and comparing the meaning of the text they are reading. These people are known as religious fundamentalists. What exactly are religious fundamentalists? The Merriam-Webster dictionary defines fundamentalism as interpreting the scriptures about the life and teaching of Jesus Christ and following the beliefs as described in the Bible.

Keep in mind that the cons of believing in religion are based on the one-sided views of fundamentalists who, in their minds, believe it to be the truth. If we have to be honest with ourselves, we all tend to have a sliver of fundamentalism in us. Your views of the cons might not be what you believe to be negative. Many of what you will read may have been taught to you during your formative years which made you believe them to be true. There are many religions and religious denominations that practice and believe in the following list.

1. People who do not believe in God will go to hell.

2. People will try to convince you that their religion will save your soul from an eternity in hell.

3. Believers are led to believe that if they commit a sin, that they will go to hell.

4. Sex before marriage is a sin.

5. Homosexuality is a sin.

6. There are religions that believe that women should be seen and not heard, implying that men are superior.

7. There are religions that condone the abuse of women and children.

8. Acts of violence, as depicted in the holy books, are taken literally by fundamentalists who participate in heinous acts and atrocities.

9. Religious fundamentalists believe that they are to eradicate the lives of people because God told them to do it.

10. There are religions that teach that people should practice abstinence or indulgence until they reach the afterlife, rather than be happy and living their lives to the best of their ability while they are alive.

11. There are religions that judge and condemn poor and needy people in their communities and the third world.

12. In the Christian faith, it is believed that Jesus' teachings are extreme.

13. It is believed that religion influences the government in many countries.

14. There are religious fundamentalists that influence voters who to vote for.

15. There are religions that do not believe in science.

The Pros of Believing in Religion

Now that we have gotten the negative side of religions and religious beliefs out of the way, it is time to explore the positive side. The positives restore faith and belief in humankind. Religion is not meant to be restricting or suffocating.

The following verses are evidence that God loved us so much that He was willing to sacrifice His Son so that our sins of yesterday, today and tomorrow will be forgiven.

"For God so loved the world that He gave His only begotten Son, that whoever believes in Him should not perish but have everlasting life," (*New King James Bible*, 1982, John 3:16).

"For Christ also suffered once for sins, the just for the unjust, that He might bring us to God, being put to death in the flesh but made alive by the Spirit," (*New King James Bible*, 1982, 1 Pet. 3:18).

1. Religion and beliefs allow people to believe that they have a purpose in life.

2. Religion allows people to believe in guidance in their lives.

3. People believe that religion gives them strength and courage to face difficult situations in life.

4. Most believers believe that things happen for a reason, especially in times when the odds are against them.

5. Most believers believe that God will guide them when they are at a crossroads in their lives.

6. Believers believe that their sins of the past are forgiven and that they do not need to feel guilty for their past transgressions.

7. Believers believe that God knows them better than anyone else, and understands what they are going through.

8. Religion teaches us that people should be kind to all people.

9. Religion teaches us that people should be helping those in need.

10. Religion teaches us that people need to forgive people who have hurt them with hurtful words or actions.

11. Religion teaches us to be humble.

12. Religion teaches us to be grateful for everything we have.

13. Religion teaches us the difference between right and wrong.

14. Religion teaches us that it is okay to not know and understand everything that is happening in our lives.

15. Focusing on what matters is more important to our lives than the expectations dictated by the world.

Ending on a High Note

For whatever reason you chose to put your hope, faith, and belief into your religion, you made a conscious choice to do what your heart led you to do. Is it bad to dedicate your life to revolve around your religion? I believe that if you are a believer that does not force your beliefs onto others, or belong to a fundamentalist religion that dictates your every move, it is not bad. There are religions that believe that you have to wear specific undergarments to remain pure and prevent you from having impure sexual urges. There are religions that believe that medical procedures such as surgeries that require blood transfusions are not of God. No matter what you believe in, you cannot force people to go against their religions, a religion they were born into.

I would like to end this chapter on a positive note, with a testimonial from a fellow believer named Sara:

During my 20s, I went on a church retreat. During this retreat, I accepted God into my heart and became a reborn Christian. I tried to live my life following the straight and narrow, believing that God was watching my every move and that I would go to hell if I wandered off the path. Although I continued to believe in God, I stopped going to church as my family had convinced me that I was becoming a fundamentalist. Was I really a fundamentalist? Looking back, I believe that I was.

I continued living my life, believing in God with the exception of not going to church. During my absence from the church, I actually found myself. I know this sounds strange, but I had a clearer vision of what God wanted from me. To this day, I believe that breaking my ties with the Methodist church was good for me. I did not agree with many of the teachings and I definitely did not agree with the sermons revolving around finances and politics.

In 2013, I lost my mother to a massive heart attack. One moment she was talking to me and the next moment she was gone. Most people would be angry and turn their backs on God after a traumatic loss, but I never did. I found that my belief in God trebled in strength. I was at peace because I believed that God would not have taken her if He thought I would not be okay. I also knew that I did everything I could for her in the last nine weeks of her life after her first heart attack.

In 2020, when the world was put on lockdown, billions of people's lives were affected by way of job losses. I was one of those people. I had debt coming out of my ears but yet I was strangely calm. Family and friends were concerned about me, but I was not. I believed God had a plan. One day, just after I had lost my job, I was scrolling through YouTube and came across Pastor Joseph Prince from the New Creations Church in Singapore. I watched one of his motivational clips. At the end of the clip, a recommendation came up with a link to his church. Thinking I had nothing to lose, I clicked on the link and set up the reminder for a church service.

From the moment he opened his mouth to start speaking, I was hooked. I recall spending an hour in tears as he spoke. I felt as if he was speaking directly to me. I should mention at this point that I suffer from severe anxiety that would leave me in agony and suffering for up to three days. After a month of joining his services, my anxiety became less and less, to the point where I did not need my medication. Now, a year after following his sermons, I count down the days to the next service. I have friends who do not like Pastor Prince because of the way he speaks—he is of Asian descent, but it never bothered me. I believe that God led me to Pastor Prince and his Church.

Thanks to Pastor Prince, I no longer view the scriptures and teachings to be literal. His teachings are backed by different versions of the Bible, such as the King James Version, the New King James Version, the New International Version, and the Hebrew teachings. Not a Sunday goes by where I turn off the recordings, where I am not or have not been crying because everything he preaches hits me square in the chest. Do I believe that God is real? Absolutely. Do I believe God loves me as I am, warts and all? Absolutely, without a doubt. If I did not believe in God, I would not be where I am today, and I would be living a life that I am not proud of. Because of God, and his love for me, doors that were closed were thrust open and I was pushed through and the doors that were open have been sealed shut, never to open again.

God is good, and all the time, God is good!

Chapter 6:

The Power of Love

Love suffers long and is kind; love does not envy; love does not parade itself, is not puffed up; does not behave rudely, does not seek its own, is not provoked, thinks no evil; does not rejoice in iniquity, but rejoices in the truth; bears all things, believes all things, hopes all things, endures all things. Love never fails. But whether there are prophecies, they will fail; whether there are tongues, they will cease; whether there is knowledge, it will vanish away (New King James Bible, 1982. Cor. 13:4-8).

Whether you want to believe it or not, your first true love is the woman who gave birth to you. The love you have for your mother cannot be compared with the love you have for another person. This statement might seem to be extreme, but take a moment to hear me out.

I realize that not everyone has happy and loving childhood memories of their mother or father. There are circumstances that are beyond our control that made us a part of this world, good or bad. Regardless of the circumstances, each of us has a love for the woman that birthed us. After all, she chose to give you life. I know that this is a controversial topic, especially where children are raised in abusive homes or given up for adoption. The bottom line is, with so many alternatives at her disposal, she chose to give you life, which indicates that your mother loved you.

I believe in forgiveness. At some point in our lives, we have to forgive people who have hurt us, either intentionally or by accident. The way I see it, we can free our hearts by forgiving. The hardened walls around our hearts, created with anger and hatred, will crumble, setting our hearts free to see the good things we had locked away.

This love story, the one between a child and their mother, is the introduction to future love. A legacy, if you want to give it a name, where we get to write our own love story and choose the characters we want in our lives. Again, there are no right or wrong questions when it comes to love. No one knows what you are thinking or feeling. Yes, you saw this one coming—love is a personal choice. Test and challenge your choices and do not settle for anything less than your perfect, not society's vision of perfect, *your* perfect.

What Is Love?

Take a moment to reflect on the idea that your love story started before you had your first cry. Is it possible to even know what love is that early on in your life? Due to my faith and beliefs, I believe that anything is possible. When a baby is born, they learn to trust their mothers to care for them by keeping them clean, warm, and fed. That trust is part of a deep love.

Is the love we see on television or in the movies a true representation of what love really is? Girl meets boy, they fall in, something happens and they break up, but when the heart wants what it wants, they end up together and they all live happily ever after. *The Notebook*, a 2004 romantic drama featuring Ryan Gosling and Rachel McAdams, is at the top of the list of most people as being one of the best love stories ever. Love, in the real world, is not all about sunshine, roses, and fluffy white bunnies.

In the real world, love is a combination of emotions and actions based on trust, desire, loyalty, affections, and caring. As your love for your partner grows, the more intense it will become until you reach the point where you either get married, move in together, or break the ties. Love also involves positive and negative emotions, which we will be covering in this chapter.

Different Types of Love

While researching this book, I came across four different types of love. The types are categorized to show the difference in the expressions, feelings, and emotions regarding an object, a situation, family and friends, or the special person in your life.

Each person has their own interpretation of love, which honestly, is perfectly fine. We are not robots and we do not have to be forced into seeing only one side of the page. We should not be influenced (or bullied) by those around us.

When looking at the different types of love, I found myself looking for comparisons across various online publications. Many of the articles I stumbled upon all featured the same type of content by separating the different types of love into categories. A Christianity expert, Jack Zavada, wrote an article about the different types of love for an online publication, *Learn Religions*. In the article, he addresses four categories that define the four types of love according to the Greeks, namely Eros, Philia, Storge, and Agape.

Eros

Eros, as we know, is the Greek god of love, but Eros has a string of meanings associated with his name that explains more about what he actually means. Possible meanings include sexual desire, and physical love, and attractions. Sex is a subject that either makes people uncomfortable or gives people an opening to tell anyone who will listen to stories of their sex life.

While many regard sex as a topic to be discussed freely, some prefer to keep their sex lives private and between the two people in the relationship. Many religions view sex before marriage as a sin, and some scriptures support these claims. I personally believe that if you are committed to your partner, and that your partner is your "forever person," then you should do what comes naturally. Before making any rash decisions, read through the entire chapter before deciding whether you are in love or lust and what your relationship is based upon.

Storge

Storge is a Greek word meaning family love. The love we have for our relatives is the foundation love is built on. It is a natural and pure love, filled with adoration for the people we spend the first 18 years of our lives with. These people, whether it be biological families or adoptive families, have loved us unconditionally. It is their love and guidance that steer us along the path of righteousness. As we get older and start our own families, we will be passing on our Storge to our children.

Philia

Philia is a Greek word meaning a type of intimate love. Not to be confused with Eros, which is about the physical love between two people. The intimate love being referred to in this instance is that of a bond between friends that have overcome many obstacles. This is a friendship that, no matter how many people have tried to sabotage, just gets stronger.

Agape

Agape is a term used by the Greeks to define God's love for us. In the scriptures that have been shared until now, you would have seen the love our Heavenly Father has for us. This is a love that does not come close to any of the other types of loves mentioned. Agape is the most perfect, most beautiful, and purest form of love for every person living on this earth. You read correctly, even the sinners are showered in Agape love.

The love God has for us is so strong that it cannot be compared to Eros, Philia, or Storge. God loves all of humankind so much that He sacrificed His Son to prove just how much He loves us. God wiped our slates clean on the day He allowed Jesus to be crucified, resurrected Him three days later, and called Him home 40 days after the resurrection. How can anyone turn their backs on a love that was given to us as a gift (Zavada, 2020)?

The Importance of Trust in a Relationship

Trust is the foundation of any relationship, whether it is with family, friends, or partners. As we mentioned, my first love and your first love is or was our mother's. As babies, without the right to choose what was best for us, we trusted our mothers to care for us. As we grew older, and the relationship between mother and child either flourished or fell apart, it does not take away from the fact that our mothers gave us life when they knew they had other options. The trust you have in a partner is the faith you have based on loyalty and love. By trusting your partner with the most vulnerable part of your existence, your heart proves to them that you feel safe knowing that they will protect you at all times.

Love Does Not Exist Without Trust

Can you justify a relationship where there is no trust? Can you entrust something as precious as your heart to someone you do not trust? Your answer to these questions should be "no." Your heart and your love is something that you hold onto until your partner proves that they are trustworthy.

Trust the Obstacles

Trust is knowing that your partner will stick by you through the good, the bad, and the testing times. Trust is earned over time and not overnight. Be vigilant and keep your heart guarded. You will know if the love that has crossed your path is real or a distraction. Remember, nobody gets love right on the first try.

Trust Is Reassuring

No relationship is perfect. This statement is not meant to affect your relationship in any shape, way or form. What I am getting to, is that every couple in a healthy relationship has the odd spat on occasion. Arguments and fights do happen but at the end of the word-slinging brawl, you can turn to each other and say, "I am sorry. I love you." Trusting your partner that they will not turn their back on you during an argument is very reassuring and indicative that you are in the relationship for the long haul.

Trust Does Not Need to Be Justified

If your relationship is one built on a foundation of trust, you will not have to explain why you are doing what you are doing. Your partner will instinctively know what you are trying to accomplish.

Trust Is Not About Jealousy

Unless you have reasons not to trust your partner, you should not allow the green monster to enter your mind. If your partner tells you they are going to be working or going out with friends, you need to put your insecurity on the backburner. It is a healthy practice for relationships to have separate interests, or to have the space to do what they want to do.

Telltale Signs of a Healthy, Trustworthy Relationship

Whether it is your first serious relationship or your sixth serious relationship, you know the trust signs and triggers. When you enter a relationship, you are distrusting, especially when you are the one that repeatedly got burnt because of trust. We are going to look at a couple of points of what to look out for when in a relationship. Some of the points might apply, some might not, but at least you will have a checklist of what to look out for until you let your guard down.

- Open and honest conversations about what is going on. This includes sharing information that might be uncomfortable to hear, but the fact that they are sharing indicates that they are trusting you and you can trust them.

- Not afraid to admit when they are wrong.

- Not afraid or embarrassed to share financial status, regardless of the state of the financial situation.

- Prioritizing your partner shows them that you are as important to them as they are to you.

- Actively listening to your partner without interruptions indicates that you have respect for them.

- Relationships are not all about sex. While public displays of affection are frowned upon, there is nothing that says you cannot hold hands while walking through the store, rubbing shoulders while watching a movie, sneaking a kiss while waiting to go into the restaurant, or brushing the hair out of your partner's eyes while enjoying a cup of coffee.

- The ultimate test that there is trust in a relationship, in my opinion of course, is when you remain focused on your partner when you are having a conversation. Dedicate the time to your partner, do not break eye contact, and remove distractions such as anything to fidget with, or mobile phones.

Emotional Intelligence: The Advantages and Disadvantages

From the time that we were able to understand yes and no and right from wrong, we were aware of the consequences of our choices. As we reached the age where we did not care to take advice from our peers, we knew that whatever choices we made would have consequences. Guess what? This is part of life. It is something we all have to figure out. Whether you are a teenager, a young adult, or a senior adult, we still make mistakes and we will carry on making mistakes because nobody and no situation is perfect.

Depending on the type of love you have, you put your heart and soul into a relationship. When things start short-circuiting, you become emotional to the point of obsessing, and before you know what is happening, you find yourself consumed with anger. Emotional intelligence is about being in touch with your innermost feelings. Although it might seem like being emotionally wise is a wonderful idea, there are several negative implications.

Advantages of Emotional Intelligence

Being emotionally intelligent helps you connect with individuals without having to express any words. There are instances where people do not like talking about their problems. This might be seen as a disadvantage rather than an advantage, but having someone who is on the same wavelength could be immensely helpful. The following advantages are examples of how emotional intelligence is measured and used to help others, or yourself.

Practice Makes Perfect

Emotional intelligence is a skill you learn over time due to circumstances or events that require you to safeguard your emotions. Depending on the situation, some people are quick studies. They can adopt and adapt the skills learned faster than others. It is not a race to see who can learn how to protect emotions faster, it is about taking the time to learn the skills and apply them to your life when you are ready.

Understanding Leads to Caring

As we start learning how to deal with and safeguard our emotions, we also learn valuable lessons about those around us. We can sense people's emotions, which although it might seem a bit intrusive, it is something that could keep us grounded. By tapping into other people's emotions, we are having a "reality check" and in turn, this will make us more in tune with what other people are going through. In other words, we are learning to be compassionate.

Logic Versus Emotions

The logical side of your brain is going to analyze and scrutinize everything before it is comfortable with taking the next steps. The emotional side of the brain is a little quicker to the ballgame, as there is not a lot of thought going into the action. The reason for this is that our emotions are tied to our everyday existence and most of the time, we do not have the time to analyze everything and therefore we have to act virtually immediately. Our brains and our hearts capture the data at different speeds, but it all gets stored in a virtual bank where it can be accessed at the drop of a hat.

Putting Our Intelligence to Work

We have the skillset to move mountains. We have the skills to apply ourselves to whatever drives our innermost passions such as hobbies, work, or sport. If you have a passion for cooking, you will sign up for classes or search through your family treasure chest of recipes and rework them to add a touch of your modern spin to it.

Disadvantages of Emotional Intelligence

Every positive has a negative, and being emotionally intelligent is no different. Where we are connected to others on a level that allows us to be supportive and understanding, there are downsides. Emotionally intelligent individuals wear their emotions and weaknesses on their sleeves, making them vulnerable to being negatively influenced or taken advantage of.

The Art of Manipulation

According to the Cambridge Dictionary, manipulation is the act of using or controlling a situation or a person to their advantage. Many people thrive on turning a vulnerable person or situation into a position where they are negatively affected. Emotionally intelligent people are easily manipulated because the manipulator preys on their senses of compassion and empathy.

I recently met a middle-aged lady that told me she has a degree in being manipulated. Her response was:

The first 10 years of my life, I was an only child. When my sibling was born, she became the center of attention, and everyone doted on her. It did not bother me, as I was always off playing by myself. I doted on my baby sister, and we all indulged her and gave in to her demands. When she reached her 20s, the wheels fell off. The verbal and mental abuse started, and she did to me what no one should ever do—and that was to steal my credit card and clean it out (it happened twice). I don't know how, I don't know when, but she twisted the whole credit card thing around by saying I gave it to her. Even now, 18 years later, she still carries on with her manipulative ways, and it does not bother her. She has successfully managed to turn family members away from me by convincing them that I want money from them.

Playing on Emotions

When people know you well enough, they know your weaknesses and use them to their advantage. A perfect example would be that someone knows you love animals and after asking you for money, and you repeatedly saying you do not have, they up the ante and tell you that their pet is very ill and needs veterinary care. They know that you will do whatever you have to do to find the funds to "pay the bill." When you follow up on how the animal is going, you start getting conflicting feedback and you start putting the pieces together and realize that you have been taken for a fool.

Personal Gain

Again, this is a form of manipulation. People are abusing your willingness to help in whatever way you can to benefit themselves. These users and abusers are narcissists and bullies who will do anything in their power to embarrass you, belittle you, and turn people against you because they are jealous of your easy-going, positive, kind, and loving nature. Most of the time it is someone close to you who does not want to see you happy or succeed in life.

Out of Context

All too often, we see or read something that makes us believe that we are the target audience. I find that social media platforms are the cause of a lot of hyped-up conflicts. It takes one person to post a status update, a quote, or a meme for someone to feel as if it is a personal attack aimed at them.

Time Taken to Develop

We know that emotional intelligence is not passed down through the generations, nor is it something that comes naturally. It is a skill you have to learn. It is a journey of discovery and perseverance, of digging into your emotions, and exposing your vulnerability. There is no timeline for the skills to develop. It is important that you do not give up, no matter what your fears, habits, or negative emotions, you need to look within your soul and make the necessary changes. After all, you want to protect your emotions and create a library for your skills.

In Summary

"'Tis better to have loved and lost than never to have loved at all."

– Alfred Lord Tennyson

Love is a four-letter word that has the ability to build you up or break you down. This chapter has been about the different types of love and the ups and downs of investing your heart into a relationship. Many are afraid of this four-letter word because they do not understand the power behind it or what it entails.

Many people pride themselves on having a hardened heart because they have been burnt one too many times. Many people have given up on love after losing a loved one or having been cheated on. Love is not only about a physical relationship between people, it is about emotions, and connecting with a person on an emotional level. Love is sharing your heart with someone who respects you as you are, and does not judge you by your indiscretions.

No matter where your heart is, always remember that God loves you. In His eyes, you are perfect. Your perfect imperfections make you unique. Yes, I am telling you, no matter who you are, God loves you and He does not see your flaws.

What Makes Love Important?

To end this chapter, I have decided to leave you with a couple of points about why having love in your life is so important. Take a moment to reflect on the points. Adopt these points to accompany you on your journey through life. Even if you have convinced yourself that you are not worthy of love or being loved, remember that God loves you, warts and all.

- Love is a tonic that breaks down the barriers of anger and hatred and allows you to forgive.

- Love is a fertilizer that nourishes your heart and soul to expand beyond the cavities in your body.

- Love is a vitamin that keeps you going, even when it seems as if all hope has been lost.

- Love is a drug that makes your heart flutter with happiness.

- Love is an antidepressant that lifts your spirits and cups your anxiety to ensure that you do not crumble under undue stress.

- Love is like a kaleidoscope that opens up to a vision of artistic abilities such as writing, cooking, gardening, or singing.

- Love is a free-thinker that accepts themselves, as well as those around them. Love is not about judging people based on their gender, the color of their skin, their religion, or the size of their bank balance.

Chapter 7:

Living in a World that is Driven by

Status

I want to open people's eyes to the reality of the world. I want readers to see how the world sees us in various settings. What we think is perfectly normal, is not necessarily the world's normal. Not everyone lives a life of privilege. Yet, many try to live up to certain expectations because that is what we see others do. We do not want to feel left out or become outcasts.

The problem is, we are living in a world where we try to out-perform each other. Instead of accepting who and what we are, we adopt the "anything you can do, I can do better" mentality. Most of the time we convince ourselves that we are living in a bubble. Nobody but those living in the bubble is important. What goes on outside the bubble has no significance whatsoever. At the end of the day, those of us living in the bubbles have successfully convinced others that we are superior and we deserve to be on the pedestal to be admired by all.

On the other hand, status is not all about privilege, wealth, or anything materialistic. It is a label that everyone has based on the way they conduct themselves in the eyes of those around them. What the labels entail is up to each individual, and you get to choose how you portray yourself to others.

I have always wondered why we, as humans, want to be someone or something that we are not. After all, God created us in His image, and in His eyes, we are perfect. Why mess with a perfect recipe? Why worry about other people's impression of you? Why allow or give people the power to judge you based on your possessions or the way you conduct yourself?

This chapter is going to be about the unrealistic expectations we have set up for ourselves. We will look at the importance of status in our lives, the downside of being dependent on status, and believing in ourselves without being concerned about the labels given to us or what others think about us. I am going to sound like a broken record, but I need to remind you to keep an open mind. As we work through this chapter, I want you to form your opinions and arrive at conclusions on your own. Remember, always be true to yourself. Be who you are meant to be and believe in yourself.

The Importance of Status in Our Lives

There are different interpretations of how status affects our lives. A majority of the people I spoke to during the research phase of this book expressed various emotions ranging from surprise and shock, to envy when telling me their interpretation of status based on watching family vlogs on YouTube. I had to remind them that what they are watching is about people flaunting what they have for popularity and clout, and the hope for endorsements from companies such as Clad & Cloth, Hello Fresh, Thrive, or Shine Cosmetics.

Why is status important in the lives of everyday people? People that just go about their day without putting on airs and graces. People who grace us with their presence and light up our lives with their smiles. People who picked up a pencil that rolled off the desk and returned it. I wonder, could it be because these people are performing selfless acts in a "normal" world and not being splashed on social media platforms looking for a pat on the back?

Status: Through the Eyes of the World

If you thought that you could float through life without being noticed, you are about to realize that people are not as oblivious to your existence and you would like to think. At the beginning of this book, you were questioning your importance in this world. You are not oblivious to the way people look at you. You feel self-confident because the last thing you want is attention. Guess what? Someone has noticed you because of something you did or said. Status labels are based on judging a person before knowing the person, whether positive or negative.

It does seem unfair to judge someone based on something they did or said, but that is the beauty of life, statuses can change once you give people an honest look at what you are about. A perfect example to use in this context; Jocelyn is someone that will go out of her way to help people. Many times, she will go without to make sure others are taken care of. It is not only her friends that benefit but strangers as well. When meeting Jocelyn for the first time, I got the fright of my life. She is a large woman. I know she saw the shock and horror on my face, but she smiled, shook my hand, and introduced herself before sitting down. Half an hour into the conversation, I was embarrassed at myself for labeling her because of her size. Before me sat a wonderful lady with a heart so pure that the light radiating from within her melts the coldest heart. This is a story that reminds you, me, and all of mankind that we should not be judging books by their cover.

Status: It Is Not Optional

You do not want the attention, you do not need the attention, and people can think what they want. You avoid eye contact, hoping that you will not be noticed. You find a spot where you hope that no one will notice you. You notice someone is crossing the room to you, and you flee in a state of panic.

The status you are labeled with in this instance is that of being arrogant. When in fact, you do not like attention or you are shy and do not know how to interact with people. We have all been there. Many people try to go through life without drawing attention to themselves, but the more that happens, the bigger the bullseye becomes. Acknowledge your status label, do not let it define you, and remain humble at all times.

Status: Positive Changes

If this book has taught you anything thus far, it is that you should be open to changes. You have nothing to lose by implementing positive changes in your life. A simple shift in the way you think, act or portray yourself is a step in the positive direction. You do not want to be known as a sulky person. Let down your guard, and allow people you meet to see the real person that is hiding behind the mask. The more you allow people to see the type of person you are, the more respect you will earn and your status in life will change.

The Downside of Being Driven by Status

There are positive effects of being labeled by statuses. Personal statuses were pointed out to help you portray yourself in a positive light. You do not want to go through life being labeled as someone you are not. Yes, you know you should not conform to what society wants from you, but you also do want people to see you.

There are instances where people go to the extreme. They change the way society views them, and they build onto that change. One can say that they become complacent and arrogant with what they have and what they can offer. A window of opportunity opens and they swoop in because they can, regardless of the consequences.

Bad Decisions

I do not believe that there are bad people in this world. People make bad choices that portray them in a negative light. Affluent people that make more money in a day than most people make in a month are using their statuses because they believe they are doing good.

An example of status over goodness erupted in 2019 with the college admissions bribery scandal, as it was labeled in all media publications.

Instead of following the correct channels and putting in the work to go to college, wealthy parents which included bankers, actresses, and fashion moguls used their status to buy their children a place in the college. Yes, we all know who is being referred to here.

The scandal opened up a can of worms that cannot ever be changed, and it is a topic that many non-affluent parents continue to talk about. Using resources to cheat their way into college has left a very bad taste in the mouths of people across the world. Understandably, parents want the best for their children, but to use their status and social standing, including their wealth, to manipulate the system is unfair to those who rightfully deserve it.

Keeping up With the Joneses

We have touched on this already, but this does require a bit more insight. No one can deny that they have tried to portray themselves as being a status-seeker. Regardless of whether they have the financial means or not, this is something that occurs more often than not.

Growing up, I was always told to live within my means. When I asked for a pair of name-brand shoes, I would be told to save up to buy it myself because I would appreciate it more having used my own money. I struggled to understand this. My friends would get what they wanted, whenever they wanted—or so I believed. I was envious because they had name-brand clothing, the latest mobile phones, 0r flashy cars. We have all experienced the desire to have the best of everything.

When I stepped out into the world, on my own, and started earning an income, I realized what my parents had been trying to teach me. One of the greatest lessons I learned was that of responsibility. Working for your paycheck makes you understand that you should not take anything for granted. Trying to live up to the expectation of society is a sure way for you to fall into a trap where you lose yourself and, well, your money. You learn to prioritize, and as my parents taught me early on in life, if you want something, you will save until you can buy it and appreciate it.

Double-Sided Religious Sword

Okay, the heading seems a little more extreme than it is going to sound, but it is a topic that is close to my heart. It is also something that I have been noticing a lot since the world went into lockdown at the end of 2019. While no one can say for certain when the global pandemic will be over, or if it will ever die out, one thing that has kept me and a lot of people going is believing that God knows what He is doing. It has been a time of belief, trust, and faith.

The issue we are faced with, which again, might not seem like an issue to many, is that people preach the good, but, in another breath, they are spewing hateful comments that go against the beliefs of believers. The people that pride themselves on the status of being believers are under the microscope. We want to surround ourselves with like-minded believers because we all have the same principles. Sadly, this is not always the case.

No one is going to say that Christians are perfect. We all make mistakes, that is part of life. However, some people do take the religious status to a level that allows people to judge all Christians based on their actions. For instance, I see good in everyone. I give everyone the benefit of the doubt. I share my testimony with as many people as I can. The problem is, not everyone is on the same page as me and that is their choice, but their choices make it difficult for people who try their best to live by the word. For this reason, everyone should always be true to themselves and what they believe in. I cannot speak for others, and I tell you why they do the things that they do. It is not my responsibility to keep them in check, and at the end of the day, they have to stand before God and answer for their actions while on this earth.

Chapter 8:

For the Love of Work

As children, we had dreams of becoming doctors, nurses, teachers, policemen, firefighters, or zookeepers. In fact, when asked what we wanted to become, these were some of the most common answers. As we got older, our choices changed. At the age of seven, we do not really know what we want to do or be. I have heard children say, when asked, that they want to be a mommy and have babies and others say that they want to be lawyers.

By the time we get to high school, we sort of have an idea of what our future might look like. Some will say that they want to go to college, while others do not feel that passion. Who really wants to spend another year or six at college after 12 years of school? This is a discussion that should happen between the student and their parents, as well as the guidance counselor. At the end of the day, everyone has to make a choice based on what their passion is.

Everyone wants to earn an income. If you did not know it before, I am about to tell you that money does not grow on trees. You cannot rely on Monopoly money to buy a car, pay the rent, or splurge on grocery hauls. I do apologize if you believed it, but I felt the calling to set the record straight. In all seriousness, the days of living off our parents should end at some point. As they advance in years, it is our turn to take care of them, and in doing that, we need to evaluate our lives.

The Importance of Working

The year 2020 is one that will be written in the history books. No matter where you are in the world, the global pandemic affected everyone. While the future is uncertain, we had to learn to adapt to the new normal. One of the biggest changes that took place was the status of our jobs. Other than the devastating effects that claimed and continues to claim the lives of people, billions of people found themselves without work. The global job market was plunged into a dark hole because of the uncertainty. We were confined to our homes and worried about where the money would come from to pay for the bare essentials, such as power, water, and food.

There were those that were fortunate enough to keep their jobs, although circumstances did change. People started working from home where Zoom and Skype became virtual boardrooms. Call center operators were given the necessary equipment so that they could continue working remotely. Instead of hearing phones ringing and distracting background noises from colleagues, we were hearing dogs barking, children laughing, or the clinking of coffee mugs. I am not saying that this happened all over the world, but listening to the people I interviewed, I sensed that the majority of workers were in agreement.

Although I cannot offer any solutions to the unemployment crisis, we can investigate why, other than the financial side, having a job is important. At this point, I would like to add that having faith and belief is important. I know it seems that all hope is lost, but if you believe, and keep on believing, something is waiting for you. Who knows, your dream job is waiting behind a closed door?

Finances

That paycheck at the end of every week or month is something we all work towards. There are bills to pay and people to feed. In short, everyone has a standard of living to maintain and a credit record that needs to be upheld.

Climbing the Ladder of Success

Most jobs offer the opportunity to follow training courses where you can build on your current qualifications. The training courses are also designed to help with skills such as customer care. Overall, by doing additional training, you will be proving to your peers that you want to learn and you want to move up in the workplace.

Distraction

A lot of people throw themselves into their work as a means of distracting them from problems they might have in their personal lives or to keep them disciplined and grounded.

Character

Working with people, whether working in an office setting or at the local fast-food restaurant, you are building your character and developing your unique personality.

Respect

Regardless of social status, people that work earn respect because of their dedication to their jobs. Healthcare workers, law enforcement, and firefighters are respected members of communities.

Your Career Is Your Whole World: Pros and Cons

At some point during your schooling career, you were told to draw up a list of goals about what you hoped to achieve when you graduated. Whether you were college-bound or not, that list became your roadmap for your future. You might have started out in the mailroom of the company in the hopes of working your way up the ladder to the desired position. You might have taken some classes at the local community college in the evenings to learn some skills. Basically, you poured all your time and energy into your work so that you could make it to a position your family and friends would be proud of.

Dedicating your life to your career might not have been intentional, but you did it because that was your passion. You never saw your dedication to your work as a sacrifice. You were working a 70-hour workweek, with little to no time for a social life. Whatever free time you had, you were thinking about work and planning the week ahead. On the rare occasion that you go out to the local bar for a drink with your colleagues, you meet someone. That someone becomes the special person in your life. You scale down on your 70-hour workweek and romance your special person. You propose, get married, and settle into a life between home and work.

Although married, work is still a priority because you have not reached the tier you want to be at, according to your goal list. Your relationship with your spouse becomes strained because you are focusing all your energy on your work and your desire to be the best. Then the ultimatums start, either me or work. At this point, you realize that something has to change.

Stacking the Pros

I know this scenario does not apply to everyone, but it is an accurate interpretation of work consuming your life. Do you believe that your work is more important than your happiness? At what point do you step back? Let us take a look at some of the pros and cons of working, whether it is in an office or remotely. These are not meant to influence you or shame you for the choices you make regarding your career or work.

Office: Discipline and Structure

If you have had problems managing your time, then working is a good option to learn discipline. Your day is structured so that you can be more productive. You know when your workday starts, you know when you can take breaks, and when your workday ends. These are the boundaries that will teach you discipline and time management.

Office: Interaction with Colleagues

If you are a hot under the collar type of person, working in an office environment teaches you to think before you act skills. You might not want to be friends with your colleagues, but you do want to get along with them. The last thing anyone wants in a job is to create conflict with your co-workers. Conflict leads to an unhealthy work environment.

Office: Experience

Whether you start your career in the mailroom or at an entry-level position in any company, there are many opportunities to grow and learn new skills. Before you know it, you will be climbing the ladder and doors will open that will see you move up in the company.

Remote: No Location Restrictions

One of the beauties of working remotely is that your work can be wherever you are, regardless of the location. If you decide to spend a week on a tropical island with your spouse, you can take your work with you. You also get to set your own working hours which are less restrictive and manageable.

Remote: Saving Money

Working remotely saves you a lot of money. You do not have to dress to impress, you do not have to buy gas or pay for wear and tear on your vehicle, and you are saving a company money by not using their equipment, power, water, or drinking their coffee.

Remote: Flexible

You can plan your day around your work schedule. If you need to go to the doctor, you do not need to worry about missing work. A leisurely lunch date with your special person or friends without worrying that you need to get back to the office.

Remote: Health

Working remotely allows you the time to take care of yourself. When you feel like the walls are closing in on you, go for a walk, work in the garden or read a book. You do not need to worry about being exposed to colds and flu when working in an office with 20 co-workers.

Unpacking the Cons

As much as you love your work, there are many negatives of loving your job too much! If you want to avoid the trappings of putting your life and soul into your work, you need to understand and take note of the following points. You can love your job, but you do need to create and maintain a healthy balance between work, home, and play.

Office: Difficulty Taking Time Off

Career-driven individuals pour their entire lives into their work. They are passionate about the work they do and find it difficult to take vacation time or a day off. They eat, breathe, and sleep for their jobs without considering that they need to separate work from personal life.

Office: Relationship Struggles

As previously mentioned, people dedicate their every being to their work that they neglect family and friends. Yes, they are passionate about their work and careers, but is throwing yourself into work healthy for relationships?

Office: No Room for Growth

If people are dedicated to their jobs or careers, they are preventing themselves from growing within the company. If you want to move up the ladder, expand your scope of expertise and open yourself up for change.

Office: Lifestyles Are Affected

This is in no way meant to be derogatory, but it is a factor when people dedicate their lives to their jobs. They spend hours on end at their desks and computers. They spend all their time cramming as many hours as possible into a workday without taking the time to walk around or get fresh air. Anyone who has worked in an office environment will tell you that they suffer from neck and back pain, as well as struggle to lose some of the extra pounds that have sneakily piled on during their careers.

Remote: Isolated

Working remotely can make people feel as if they are alone. There is no one to bounce ideas off of. There is no one to call out to if they are stuck on an issue.

Remote: Homelife Distractions

Many people I have spoken to have said that working in an office is distracting because there are always people talking, moving around, or phones constantly ringing. Unfortunately, working remotely presents with similar distractions. While working, they might notice that there is a dirty spot on the floor that needs to be cleaned, they are just getting started to focus on their work when the dogs start barking, or a friend pops in for a quick cup of coffee.

As with working in an office environment and the dedication, working remotely is just as bad, if not worse. In an office setting, people can leave their work on their desks but remote workers have their work 24 hours a day. They struggle to find the off switch because they feel guilty about being "selfish."

Do Not Compromise Your Beliefs for Your Career

When you enter the job market, you are excited about the new beginnings. You know where you want to be in your career, and you strive for nothing but the best. You love your work, and you will do just about anything to work yourself to a top position. Along the way, you lose focus on what you learned as a child. The healthy balance between life and work becomes clouded. Relationships suffer because you are focused on wanting to be the best, earning a salary that does not compare to friends or family, and overall, an unhealthy obsession for something that can end in a heartbeat.

One day, you feel that something is missing from your life, and you start reassessing what you believed was your dream job. You notice the people around you. The way they interact with each other might not be as healthy as you once thought it was. Your blurred vision starts clearing as you realize that you need to make changes or risk losing yourself even further.

When you started working, you had a list of goals you wanted to achieve, and you put your hopes and beliefs into that list. As you tick off the goals you have achieved, another realization hits you square in the chest, one that makes you realize you were putting your faith in a job that made you selfish, uncaring, and cold-hearted. You remember the relationships you terminated because you did not have the time for anyone other than your greedy need to succeed, regardless of the costs involved. You once believed in yourself when no one else did and you accomplished something that no one else believed you could.

Signs of Idolizing Your Job

When your life revolves around your work, you are worshipping your work before worshipping God. In your eyes, work is more important than God, family, and friends. We have established that having a job is a necessity, as an income is necessary to provide for living expenses. Again, it is not wrong to love your job and want to succeed, but placing your job on a pedestal above all others in your life, you are compromising your beliefs.

One of the Ten Commandments teaches us that we should not worship anyone or anything other than God: "You shall have no other gods before Me" (*New King James Bible*, 1982, Exod. 20:3). Here are a couple of questions you can ask yourself when thinking about where you are in life. There are no right or wrong answers, these are merely signs where your job becomes the center of your universe.

You know you are idolizing your job when you:

- Spend more time with your colleagues, outside of work hours, than friends and family.

- Talk about your work life at home, or when out to dinner with friends.

- Tell people what you do for a living when meeting them for the first time.

- Fear losing your job, leaving you without a means to support your lifestyle, and loss of income.

- Decline invitations to meet up with friends or attend social gatherings with family because of work.

If any or all of these statements resonate with you, then it is time to re-evaluate your goals. No job is worth losing who and what you are. Take the time to analyze your beliefs. Even if you do not believe in God, believe in what you think is right. Consider your family and friends. Think about where you want to be in five, 10, or 20 years. Would you rather be earning less money and be with your special person? Or, would you rather be unhappy, working, and possibly have a divorce or two on your belt?

Chapter 9:

For the Love of Money

There is so much to say about money that it is difficult to pick a starting point. What can I tell you about money that you do not already know? That is the million-dollar question. Money is something everybody loves, wants, and needs. Having money keeps food on our tables, power to our homes, clothes on our bodies, and is pretty much the beginning and end of our existence. However, money is not as freely available as we would like. The truth of the matter is, if you want money, you have to work for it because it does not grow on trees, as much as wished it would.

Instead of rambling on about money, or the lack thereof, I am going to share part of an email I received. The writer is a lady named Nelia. I do believe that this letter will pave the way for the rest of this chapter. This letter spoke to me in more ways than I can explain. The faith, belief, and devotion I felt were incredibly strong and very heartwarming.

Like most of the people in my community, and across the world, I lost my job before COVID-19 lockdowns. I had been working remotely for the last 10 years, first as a transcriptionist that managed a team of typists, and then as a copywriter for a travel agency based in South Africa. I was with the travel agency for two years. I should have had the foresight to see what was coming. In December 2019, when Covid-19 flattened China and Europe, the work started slowing down. Instead of being forthright with their workers—we were a team of five ladies scattered across the globe—they kept telling us that we do not have to worry, we would always have work.

The reassurance is meant to give you peace of mind, but as we begged for our lists to be updated so that we could work, the entire on-site team went silent on us. Emails were ignored. Text messages were ignored. December was a very difficult month for us because our $500 salaries had plummeted to approximately $150 to $200. January came along, and suddenly the work poured in again. At this point, I was keeping a close eye on the news reports and following what was going on in Italy. As they drowned us in work, a very sneaky email appeared in our inboxes—yes, if you guessed that it was a termination of contract notices, you would be correct. They were getting rid of their most productive and hardest working team. Not once did our supervisors reach out to us; all communication ceased to exist.

From earning a decent amount of money to suddenly earning nothing was a shock to my system. My anxiety attacks were intense, to the point where I was convinced that I was having a heart attack at least once a week. The phone calls from the debt collectors were the worst. I felt alone and I had no one to talk to. For about nine months, I had no income whatsoever and I was receiving food parcels from charity organizations. That is when I decided that things needed to change. I opened my heart in prayer and told God that I was at his mercy. I had nothing to lose, and a whole lot to gain by putting my faith and trust in Him.

Within three weeks, a job I applied for contacted me and invited me to an online interview. I was given instructions, did the test I needed to do, and a week later I was accepted. For me, being kept busy was more important than the lack of money and food in my home. If my mind was busy, nothing else seemed to matter. When I received my first paycheck, I immediately took 15% of that money and gifted a friend in need. Don't get me wrong, my first paycheck after 10 months of no income was hardly enough to see me through the month, but God has placed it on my heart to share. Since doing that, which is something I do not talk about because I do not want any praise, I have been blessed in more ways than I can name.

I am still struggling as I try to find my feet in my new job, and weeks go by when I do not have money or food, but God provides. One thing I have had to learn was that God works on His time and not when I want Him to. One of the biggest lessons I have learned is that God wants us to believe and trust in Him. When I feel like the world is spinning out of control, I lay all my woes at the foot of the cross and walk away. There are times when I am tempted to go back and work out a problem on my own, but I have learned to let go, and let God. My belief and faith have not let me down, and God gives me what I need when I need it. No matter what I have done in the past, God loves me for who I am and not what I was.

The Importance of Having Money

Contrary to what you may believe, money cannot buy you love and happiness. If you want to get technical, money can buy you items that will make you happy, or gifts that will make your special person love you, but what are you without money? We saw the situation Nelia was in, no income and no means to support herself and relying on charity organizations to put food on her table. She also mentioned something very important about not having money, and that was that debt collectors were phoning wanting their money.

Nelia is one of the billions of people that is walking through troubled financial waters. Some people have lost their homes and have had to move in with family or shelters because they are destitute. Children go to school hungry, and if it was not for feeding schemes at the schools, they would starve. Society looks down on people who have nothing. Having an abundance of money is a status symbol.

Why is having money important if it cannot buy you happiness, love, or a place in heaven? Money is important for you, me, and the entire human race to have what is needed to survive. Money is needed to pay for accommodation, food, healthcare and insurance, education, and the bare necessities. We are not all Mark Zuckerberg's, Bill Gates', or Elon Musk's—we are everyday people who just want to provide for our families to the best of our abilities.

Money: The Good and the Bad

Let us create a little scenario here to set the scene for this section. You buy a lottery ticket. If you do not have a ticket, you do not have a chance and your odds are one in 302.5 million (*Huddleston Jr.*, T, 2021). Have you ever considered what you would do if you won the jackpot? How would it change your life? Do you believe you would be happier knowing that you have more money than you ever dreamed of having? Let us look at how winning the jackpot can affect your life.

For the Good of Money

Financial Independence

If you are financially independent, you do not have to stress about living from paycheck to paycheck. You will have the freedom to live wherever you choose, have the finances to indulge in a weekend away, or buy the Oculus you have been wanting.

Making Dreams a Reality

If you had money, you would be able to buy the lakeside property you want to build your dream house on, take a family vacation to Cancun, Mexico, or start a business by buying the first donut franchise in your city.

Security

Having money in the bank would give you a sense of security knowing that in an emergency, you will not have to worry about where the money will come from.

Helping Those in Need

Every community has a family or families that need a helping hand. Having money would allow you to do good by buying groceries, supporting a charity, or donating pet food to the local animal shelter.

For the Bad of Money

Unhealthy Obsession

When the idea of having money consumes your life, it will create an unhealthy obsession that can create more problems than what it is worth. This obsession can lead to lying, stealing, and guilt-tripping people into giving towards your cause. People that are obsessed with money tend to create rifts amongst friends and family. I cannot speak for anyone else, but I spoke to someone who told me that a family member seems to have a sixth sense when they have money and harasses them and makes up all kinds of elaborate excuses as to why they need the money.

Family Conflict

The obsession for money, or how to spend it, may cause problems within the family because not everyone is on the same page about what is needed.

Addiction

The possibility exists that when you have money, you could use your resources to indulge in abusing substances such as drugs and alcohol or gambling. It is important to remember that addiction is not defined to people with money, but it is worthwhile to mention it under the downside of having money.

Not Very Charitable

In the previous section, we saw that when people have money, they want to help those who are in need. The downside of having money makes people less charitable because their greed and need for more drive them to be selfish. They do not want to part with their money, and any requests for assistance fall on deaf ears.

Allowing Money to Compromise Beliefs

I thought it fitting to add a separate section looking at how our obsession for money infringes on our beliefs. By now you know that money is something we need. That is a fact no one will deny. It is not bad to be wealthy, and it is nothing to be ashamed of if you have nothing. Our attitudes towards money is what is important. Yes, you earned that money by working for it, and you get to decide how you use it. No one is going to take that away from you.

When you start idolizing your money, you forget some of the principles you were taught growing up. Have faith, hope, and belief. When you are obsessing about money, or anything else, you push God to the side. Why, when people have nothing, do they put their faith in God and trust that He will provide? God wants us, He really does, to rely on Him for all our needs. Prayers are not always answered in the timely manner we want, but He does answer us when His time is right.

Losing Sight of God

Have you ever noticed that when you are in trouble or want something, you pray and ask God for help? I am almost certain that all believers, and even non-believers, call out to God for help on occasion. The moment we have what we want, we push God to the side. Many will disagree with this statement, but I have been guilty of that at times. I tell myself that I have everything I need, I am okay for now, and I do not need anything else. Until the day everything goes wrong and I find myself begging for God's intervention.

The obsession with idolizing money is such an example. We focus on the wants and not the needs. We become selfish and cling to our money as if our lives depended on it. We lose our focus on what we believe, and who we put all our trust in to indulge in our obsessions. God does not expect you to share your wealth, but he also does not want you depending on your money. What is going to happen to the money when you die? It certainly cannot be used where you go, and it cannot buy you a spot in the heavenly realm.

Do Not Lose Sight of Yourself

Then God said, "Let Us make man in Our image, according to Our likeness; let them have dominion over the fish of the sea, over the birds of the air, and over the cattle, over all the earth and over every creeping thing that creeps on the earth." So God created man in His own image; in the image of God He created him; male and female He created them. Then God blessed them, and God said to them, "Be fruitful and multiply; fill the earth and subdue it; have dominion over the fish of the sea, over the birds of the air, and over every living thing that moves on the earth," (*New King James Bible*, 1982, Genesis 1:26-28).

When you lose sight of yourself, you are turning your back on your Creator. When you had nothing, you were humbled and grateful for what you had. The fact that you did not have any money did not bother you because you knew that in the eyes of God, you were the wealthiest person alive. All of a sudden, you come into money and your beliefs jump ship because now you really are wealthy. Your attitude changes towards people, and you become the person you despise when remembering those that flaunted their wealth. Again, no one will deny you your wealth, but you are denying God by placing Him on the back burner while you let your money consume you. Be the person you truly are. When you put your belief in the money you have, or the assets you own, you are showing everyone that what you have is more important than everything else. Remember, money cannot buy you a place in heaven. Before you idolize the money you have in your bank account, read the following Bible verse, and think about how you want to be remembered as: "For the love of money is a root of all kinds of evil, for which some have strayed from the faith in their greediness, and pierced themselves through with many sorrows," (*New King James Bible*, 1982, 1 Tim. 6:10).

Chapter 10:

Finding the Good In Your Habitual

Lifestyle

Have you ever encountered people who are afraid to change their way of thinking, their habits, or their routines because they are "set in their ways?" Whether we care to admit it or not, we can compare ourselves to robots because our daily existence revolves around doing things automatically. Where some people have schedules and routines to help them keep track of their daily lives, others seem to be on auto-pilot. What we might have considered being a psychological disorder, such as obsessive-compulsive disorder (OCD), is probably a result of habits we have adopted.

What we want to do, or attempt to do in this chapter, is to change our habits to break the robotic mentality we have come to believe is part of our lives. Changes in lifestyle or way of thinking is a scary thought, especially if it is something you have been doing since you were a child. Do not let the fear of change consume you. You are not a robot that has to follow the same routine day in and day out, you are allowed to venture outside of your invisible snow globe. Take a couple of deep breaths before you re-evaluate your goals and aspirations. You can do it. I can do it. We can all do it. Neil Armstrong said, "That's one small step for a man, one giant leap for mankind," (Armstrong, 1969).

What do you say? Nothing ventured, nothing gained. Let us take a leap of faith together and believe that we can break the habitual mold that keeps us prisoner.

Re-Evaluating Goals

In "Chapter 1: You Are Important," I told you to get a journal. I then told you that you need to have goals and that everyone needs to have goals. These goals did not have to be anything dramatic, just a list of what you want to accomplish in a day, a week, or a month. I personally believe in having a list of goals. I have four different types of goal lists namely, a daily to-do list, a weekly need to-do list, a monthly accomplished list, and a bucket list of what I would like to do when the opportunity presents itself. I am not going to lie, I fail at my daily and weekly lists often, but I do adhere to my monthly and bucket lists.

Having a list of goals helps with keeping you motivated. It is something to work towards and when accomplished, you will feel proud of yourself for doing something you never thought you could. The downside to having goals is that if you do not achieve that goal, you are left feeling despondent and frustrated. I am here to tell you that not everyone achieves their goals and that is okay. The goals you have are goals you want to work towards and no matter how long it takes, you will achieve those goals. All you need is a double-dose of belief and faith in yourself.

S.M.A.R.T Goals Concept

SMART goals were developed in 1981 by George Doran, Arthur Miller, and James Cunningham, in an article titled "There's a S.M.A.R.T way to write management goals and objectives" (Doran et al., 1981). The SMART goal setting concept can be used in companies, corporations, students, or personal capacities.

S.M.A.R.T

- Specific: The intention of what you want to achieve

- Measurable: What you want to see, hear, and feel when reaching your goals

- Achievable: Believe that you will achieve your goals

- Realistic: Setting goals that are relevant to you

- Time-related: Adding a time frame could hold you accountable to achieve your goals

Goal Problems

While having goals is a good idea to help keep you focused, there are some downsides. Do not allow your goals to become an obsession to the point where your focus is on achieving them. You will be setting yourself up for failure if you do not reach your goals, which is demotivating to everyone with high expectations. Sometimes, there are circumstances beyond your control that see you falling short.

I Have Achieved My Goal—What Now?

Your goal was to lose 40 pounds. You achieved your goal within six months. As a reward, you go to Raising Cane's and order a helping of Texas Toast, a double helping of Cane's Sauce, chicken fingers, and a diet soda. The celebratory reward could possibly re-awaken your original goal.

My Goal Is to Have My Car Repaired

A pretty achievable goal, except finances have not been favorable. You are putting money aside each month. You finally have the exact amount you need. Your tooth breaks and you have to use your money to pay for an emergency dentist visit. Your hopes of ever having your car repaired are shattered. You are demotivated and frustrated. What should you do? Put it back on the goal list and start the whole saving process again.

Examples of Goals

- I want to exercise, whether walking, dancing, or going to the gym.
- Saturdays and Sundays are screen-free days.
- I want to dedicate one day a month to do volunteer work at the animal shelter.
- I want to wake up earlier to do yoga.
- I want to learn how to sew.
- I want to do a social media detox on weekends.
- I want to do an online course.

Goals can be anything you want, and there are no limits. If you find it difficult to commit to a long list of goals, start with one goal and work towards achieving it.

How Do Habits Affect Your Life?

Habits are a collection of automatic responses, rituals, and behaviors that form part of our daily lives. Using the robot and auto-pilot example, we do things without thinking about doing it, or why we are doing it. What we were taught as children have remained with us into our adult lives. Most habits are imprinted in our memories, and what you might consider to be obvious, such as brushing your teeth, is a habit that you adopted when you cut your first tooth. Our brains are a storage facility that saves all the habits we have picked up over the years, months, weeks, or days. Each time we do something, it goes into our brain and waits there until we do it again until it becomes a habit.

The habits we have adopted play an important role in our lifestyle. Thinking back over the years, you have to admit that not all your habits were good ones. When you discovered that your bad habits were negatively influencing your life, you worked to change it into a positive one.

Advantages and Disadvantages of Developing Habits

Advantages

- Habits allow us to function without putting much thought into our actions.

- Habits do not take extra time or bother because the actions are second nature.

- Habits are automatic rituals that do not need us to make decisions.

- Habits are actions that allow us to perform multiple tasks at once, such as talking on the telephone, cooking, and keeping an eye on the children.

- Having good habits sets our minds at ease and surrounds us in comfort.

Disadvantages

- Habits tend to control your life, such as drinking and smoking

- Habits can stunt your creativity and free-thinking.

- Old habits do not like it when we learn new things.

- Habits tend to control your actions.

- Habits stand between what we do and what we should be doing.

Re-Defining Your Habits to Improve Your Life

At times, a little adjustment here, a tweak there, and an overhaul all over is needed to break the cycle of habit. The older generation might agree that when practicing a habit for over 50 years, it is difficult to change the way they trained their minds. Change is never easy, it can be scary and intimidating, but at the end of the day, it gives you the chance to create new and even better habits.

Consider adding some of your old habits to your list of goals. Believe in yourself, knowing that a change has to start with you. No one can force you to change, only you can. If you want a bit of supernatural help and intervention, read the Bible for affirmation, and do not be afraid to ask God for guidance. Open your mind, and know that you have the power to make positive changes.

Positive Affirmations

Start your day by looking at yourself in the mirror. Greet the person you see with a big smile and give yourself a compliment. If you have a spare moment, share your plans for the day and give yourself an encouraging message. Not only will you be forming a new habit, but you are also changing the old habit by altering your usual morning routine.

Kindness

Treat others as you want to be treated. If they are rude to you, that is not an invitation for you to be rude to them. Do not allow people to influence you negatively. Walk away from the situation with a smile on your face. Even though you are hurting on the inside, do not give people the satisfaction of seeing your hurt and disappointment. Being kind is not about buying gifts. We have already learned that money cannot buy happiness. By saying something nice, you are spreading happiness and positivity.

Life Lessons

Life lessons are little hidden gems that appear when you least expect them. I look at these obstacles as God's way of sending me a message. I might not understand the message at that moment, and that I need to be patient, but the message is always revealed. No matter what you are faced with, good or bad, acknowledge the situation and keep an open mind. Life lessons are meant to happen at a time when you need a little shake-up or affirmation that you are doing something right. Life lessons could also be preparing you for something bigger than you expected, like a career change or meeting someone you will spend the rest of your life with. Acknowledge and embrace every obstacle that comes your way.

Decluttering

Whenever you walk into a room, your eye catches knickknacks gathering dust, books that your grandmother gave you that you have just left in a corner, broken toys that the children insist they are playing with, or whatever is out of place. Your instincts are to sell, give away or throw in the trash can but instead of dealing with it, you walk out of the room. Consider adding another goal to your list at this point, dedicating seven days to either clear a room of items you do not like, have no use for, or broken, and start decluttering. If, after seven days, you notice an improvement, go for round two. Continue with your clean-out until you are satisfied. Not only is decluttering good for the aesthetics of the home, but it will also benefit your soul. As a bonus, you are forming a new habit.

Learn a New Skill or Hobby

So often we get caught up in life that we forget to take care of ourselves. It is time to change that and make time for yourself. Learn a new skill, something you have always wanted to do but never had the courage. Whether it is learning how to make hot chocolate bombs, bath bombs, building a birdhouse, or hydroponic gardening, find something that resonates with you and keep on perfecting your skill or hobby. Who knows, you might become an entrepreneur when you start selling your wares on Etsy.

Turn Your Back on Bad Habits

Bad habits are hard to break. It is not a sign of weakness to have developed those bad habits. Difficult circumstances and situations might have led you to adopt those habits in the first place. The good news is, there is hope to break those bad habits. The best news of all is that you do not have to be ashamed of whatever is holding you hostage. We are not going to go into detail about bad habits, as we have all experienced them, but just know that there is no shame or judgment over you.

Chapter 11:

Observing Lifestyle Choices: Diet and Exercise

Jamie Ballard, a Data Journalist for YouGov, wrote an article titled "Exercising and sticking to a healthy diet are the most common 2021 New Year's resolutions." In the article, Jamie conducted a survey featuring 1,500 US adults to find out what their New Year's resolutions would be for 2021. Not surprisingly, the statistics show that 50% were going to exercise more, 48% were going to make weight loss a priority, and 39% intended to change their diets (Ballard, 2020).

Exercise, weight loss, and diet change are among the most popular New Year's resolutions when it comes to health and well-being. I would be too afraid to make a resolution knowing that friends, family, or colleagues will watch my every movement. There is nothing worse than being placed under a magnifying glass and being judged by what you are consuming, and then having to be told that what you are doing is not a good idea.

I do believe that decisions and choices about your health and wellbeing are personal. Unless a nutritionist, general practitioner, or a dietician raises concerns, you should not be letting people dictate what you should or should not be consuming, nor make you feel insecure about your choices.

Diet: When the Love of Food Becomes an Obsession

Food, along with air, water, sleep, and shelter, forms part of a list of the basic needs for humans to survive. Food can be categorized into six basic groups according to the recommendations from the United States Department of Agriculture and the United States Department of Health and Human Service. The guide, commonly known as the "food pyramid," is used to indicate the different food groups, as well as the daily recommendations per group. The guide and serving recommendations are:

- Fats, oils, and sweets: Sparingly

- Milk, cheese, and yogurt: Two to three servings per day

- Solid proteins such as animal products, legumes, and nuts: Two to three servings per day

- Vegetables: Three to five servings per day

- Fruit: Two to four servings per day

- Carbohydrates such as bread, pasta, cereal, and rice: Six to 11 servings per day (Dietary Guidelines for Americans, 2000)

If you have been around the diet block, you will know that there are hundreds of different types of diets. Not every diet is approved by members of the medical or nutritional profession. Quick-fix diets are known as fad diets. There are celebrity-endorsed diets; there are low-carb diets. The lists are endless. If you are considering a dietary lifestyle change, do your research and consult your doctor, nutritionist, or dietician.

Do Not Judge a Book by Its Cover

One of the biggest causes of concern for me has to be witnessing adults belittle children—not even their children—because they carry a couple more pounds than they should. This is not okay with me. Nobody knows what is going on in the other person's life. Nobody knows why someone is larger than normal. It is easier to judge the book by its cover rather than read the contents before passing judgment. For all you know, that person you insulted could be on life-saving medication or suffering from the trauma of losing a loved one.

These are bullies, and they do not understand that their words are what cause people to have unhealthy obsessions with food. If you are going to constantly make remarks or point out that people should consider losing a couple of pounds, they are forcing people to view food as the enemy. How many times have you done the opposite of what someone has told you to do? Probably more often than you can count. These people that get their daily dose of "I am holier than thou" fixes by pointing out the weaknesses in others are doing more harm than good. Constantly referring to someone's weight or the food they eat, they are creating a bigger problem. They are unintentionally forcing the subject of their torture to opt for an even unhealthier lifestyle.

Pros and Cons of Dieting

The word "'iet" has various meanings according to the Merriam-Webster Dictionary. The most common meaning of diet is associated with controlling the food consumed to lose weight. Diet also refers to dietary lifestyle programs such as the ketogenic diet, a vegan diet, or a low-fat diet. We can agree that diet refers to the consumption of food, regardless of restrictions or types. I am not here to tell you how to live your life or what you should be eating. It is your body, your life, and your choices. Let us take a look at some pros and cons relating to the food we consume.

Pros

- Altering your diet can relieve ailments such as food allergies or assist with autoimmune disorders

- The biggest bonus of following a diet is the weight loss involved

- Boosts and builds self-confidence

- Life expectancy is improved

- Conscious about the food you consume

Cons

- Reaching weight loss goals are difficult and may be discouraging

- A dietary lifestyle change can cause depression, especially when you do not reach the desired results

- Nutrient deficiency

- Mood swings and stressful

- Your mind could play tricks on you by telling your that you are hungry more often than normal

Food Scarcity Leads to Food Obsession

We know that we need food to survive. Many people view food to be the root of unhealthy eating habits that lead to obesity and other food-related issues. I am here to tell you that food is not the enemy. The problem steps in when food becomes the object of obsession. For instance, when you start following a healthy eating plan, you are reminded that you cannot consume your favorite foods and you find yourself thinking about it all the time.

I am sharing the following testimonial because it is an insider's perspective of an introduction to the unhealthy obsession with food. When reading this, do not be too quick to judge, and have an open mind to what is going on in your community. The fear of being without food is very real. From third-world countries to first-world countries, the topic of food scarcity pops up. Nobody will understand the fear of not having food until it happens to them.

Before my state went into lockdown, I was watching some YouTube family vloggers based in Utah. Utah seems to be the Mormon capital of the world because all the family vloggers I watch are members of The Church of Jesus Christ of Latter-day Saints (LDS). I was watching in awe as these families went from Costco to Target, to Sam's Club to stock up on food, water, and toilet paper. What shocked me the most was seeing their massive food storage rooms in their basements. To be honest, seeing their food storage rooms made me look at my own pantry which is barely bigger than a broom closet, and where their shelves were buckling under the weight, my three cubbyhole shelves were empty. You see, along with everything else going on, I did not have the finances to go shopping to fill up my little pantry.

While watching everyone panic about getting their food storages filled up, I remembered something I would much rather have forgotten. I was obsessed with food from a very early age. In my family, if you did not finish every crumb on your plate, you were made to feel guilty because of all the hours, love, and sweat that went into preparing the meal. The obsession grew with me as I got older, but it became a little more complicated. Where I was forced by the cook to mop up my plate, I started a new obsession, and that was the fear of running out of essentials. I would suffer anxiety attacks when discovering I was down to two rolls of toilet paper—knowing that they would last a week. This was and is a tough one to break free of, and if I have to be honest, I am still struggling today.

This fear spilled over to my treats and snacks. When I bought snacks with my monthly groceries, the intention was that it would go into the pantry and wait around until I wanted a treat. Yeah, that did not work out so well because of my obsession, I started devouring my treats in one sitting, saving nothing. My obsession with food, or the fear of not having any food, caused many problems for me, both mentally and physically. I tried to deal with my obsession but it was not as easy as one would think. Oh, I used to get the power is in your hands, you can do anything you set your mind to or whatever little mantra someone would throw my way.

One day I realized that if I wanted to deal with this problem, I had to free myself. In order for that to happen, I had to acknowledge that I had a problem. Until I acknowledged that I had an obsession, I was bound by the shackles of food. I started praying because I needed willpower. Within the first week of starting a new diet plan, I had lost 15 pounds. To date, I have lost a total of 87 pounds in 10 months. I have been set free. –Joanne, 48

All Your Hope Is in Food

Why do people turn to food for comfort? Food does not talk back. Food does not discriminate. Food can make you feel happy and warm. Food has been around since the beginning of times, the apple that Eve ate in the Garden of Eden is evidence. Today, food is used as a coping mechanism. It is easier to hide our emotions when hiding behind a giant bag of crisps. Emotional eaters use food as a mask to hide the pain and anguish they are going through, whether it is depression, a stressful situation, or an illness.

Food is also used as a tool to manipulate people. Whether it is offering food as a reward for doing something or an "I scratch your back, you scratch my back" scenario—food is being used as a reward system. You get the foodies that love food and they will eat because they want to. They do not care about what they are eating, nor do they care about what they are doing to their body as long as they can eat. One can even go as far as to say that they idolize their food.

On the extreme opposite side of the pole, you have those that take dieting to the extreme. They have seen what losing weight is like, and they have heard the praises that they have been given, and they stop eating because instead of worshipping food, they are now worshipping their bodies at the expense of their health. These examples may all seem far-fetched, but unless you have experienced any or all of these trials and tribulations, you will not know what people are going through. I can tell you that gluttony is real and leads to over-eating, obesity, and a whole host of health issues. Gluttony is described as an overindulgence of food and beverage being consumed. Even the Bible cautions us against gluttony by saying, "Do not mix with winebibbers, Or with gluttonous eaters of meat; For the drunkard and the glutton will come to poverty, And drowsiness will clothe a man with rags," (*New King James Bible*, 1982, Proverbs 13:20-21).

No matter what you are going through in life, have faith and hope, and believe. Even if you do not believe in a higher power, believe that you are greater than whatever problems you have. Be the person you are meant to be, strong, courageous and gorgeous.

Fitness: When the Love of Exercise Becomes an Obsession

We have taken an in-depth look at the struggles people could experience during their dietary lifestyle journey. What is health and wellbeing without throwing in some exercise? Exercise is something people love to hate and not everybody likes exercising. Regardless of how you feel, exercise is a necessary evil to keep our bodies supple and to ensure the blood flows to all the right places.

I get that not everybody likes going to a busy gym, nor do they like putting their bodies on display to be scrutinized by the already trimmed and toned Adonis or Adonia. No one can force you to do anything you do not want to do, so instead of signing up for a gym membership, consider joining up with one of the many online fitness groups that offer classes via video or Zoom.

The best gift you can do for yourself is to get out and move. Whether you dance, vacuum clean, sweep, fold the laundry, run up and down the stairs in your home, or work in the garden—you are getting your body to move. Make yourself some goals, little ones, and add to your goal list. Before you know it, you will be a pro at whatever you set out to do.

When Fitness Becomes an Obsession

While exercise is necessary to some degree, it is important not to fall prey to the traps of exercising with the intention of worshipping your body. Yes, it is wonderful that you are firming and toning your abs, and building muscles, but there comes a point where exercising becomes an addiction. I will share some examples that will give you an indication that your fitness regime went from being healthy to your idol.

- You are addicted to exercise.

- You might view your body as not being good enough, and therefore exercise more intensely and more often.

- The obsession to exercise can lead to problems between spouses or partners due to the incessant exercising and time spent at the gym.

- Where people are following healthy eating plans to lose weight, they join up with fitness programs to tone up muscles and tighten loose skin. What is not spoken about is that when the dieter steps on the scale, they will be despondent because their weight has sky-rocketed. The reason for this is that exercising builds muscle, and muscle weighs more.

- The price you pay to exercise could lead to joint damage and inflammation (Greenfield, n.d.).

In Summary

"Or do you not know that your body is the temple of the Holy Spirit who is in you, whom you have from God, and you are not your own? For you were bought at a price; therefore glorify God in your body and in your spirit, which are God's," (*New King James Bible*, 1982, Cor. 6:19-20).

Two of the most important elements that contribute to the health and wellbeing of our bodies are diet and fitness. There is a fine line between taking care of our bodies and letting our bodies go. On the one hand, we worship our bodies by exercising, and not eating for fear of undoing the work that has been done, and on the other hand, we have the "I do not care" attitude which are those that sloth around and have no self-respect for themselves. Do not compromise your beliefs by worshiping your body as if it was an idol, and do not treat your body like a second-hand vehicle.

Chapter 12:

For the Beauty of Sleep

Sleep is a precious commodity that everyone needs to remain healthy. Everyone loves to sleep. Sleep is something every parent wishes for their babies, especially the first three months of their lives when sleep is as elusive as the pot of gold at the end of the rainbow. New parents can say goodbye to the days of uninterrupted sleep. If you are not a parent yet, enjoy all the sleep you can get while you can. Sleep becomes a memory as parents watch their children grow up, but parents do not mind the deprivation that accompanies parenthood. All that matters to them is that their children are safe.

Sleep is something that should not be taken advantage of. Some people would love to get the required hours of sleep per night that are not fortunate enough. Sleep is a luxury that many people abuse. There are many types of sleep disorders that prevent people from getting the necessary rest their bodies require to function at an optimal level.

The Importance of Sleep

As mentioned in the previous chapter, diet and exercise is important to our health and wellbeing and make up two out of three components to ensure that our bodies function. The third component is sleep. Together, the three essential components work together to make sure that our bodies function to the best of their ability. Of course, as with diet and exercise, sleep does not occur naturally for a lot of people.

Sleep is vitally important as it allows your body to rest for a certain amount of time each day. During the rest period, your body has a chance to recharge and heal after a busy day of work or activities, as well as prepare for the next day. Many people do not agree that sleep is important, and they will proudly boast that they can go without sleep for long periods of time. Some even joke that all they need to get through the day is an intravenous caffeine drip. And of course, some people drink copious amounts of strong, black coffee or energy drinks to stay awake. What these people, those that believe they are invincible, do not realize is that they are harming their bodies.

Benefits of a Good Night's Rest

If your parents were anything like mine, bedtime was 7:30 p.m. and lights out by 8:15 p.m., and no amount of bartering could buy us an extra 30 minutes to finish a chapter or finish writing in our journals. I do realize now that by having a proper routine, one where parents were stricter and did not allow certain distractions such as televisions in the bedrooms or no sugary treats half an hour before going to our rooms. There was also the restriction of reading a book, writing in a journal, or doing something that would not hype us up before going to sleep.

Joe Leech, an Australian dietician published an article titled "10 Reasons Why Good Sleep is Important" for the online publication, *Healthline*. The article was medically reviewed by Atli Arnarson, who holds a Ph.D. in nutrition, obtained at the University of Iceland.

Weight Control

Good sleep, diet, and exercise equal a healthy body. Thus, people that get sufficient sleep eat less during the awake cycle of their day than those that are sleep deprived. The person who is struggling to sleep has the urge to eat more due to overactive hormones that increase the appetite. While overeating can be linked to weight gain and issues such as obesity, a good night's rest will help regulate the hormones to curb snacking during the awake cycle.

Reduced Health Risks

If you get sufficient sleep, the chances of suffering from a stroke or heart disease are reduced. A bad sleeper has an increased chance of suffering from any health issues, such as chronic diseases and heart attacks.

Depression

Depression does not choose who it is going to affect, and it depends on the situation. It is believed that getting sufficient sleep does help by minimizing the effects of depression. However, depression also plays a role in not being able to sleep or get the quality of sleep that is required.

Emotions and Interactions

It is believed that insufficient sleep affects your ability to have a conversation or social interaction with other people. In other words, if you were to get the right amount of sleep, you would feel more confident when engaging in conversation with people around you (Leech, 2020).

Reduce Stress and Improves Mood

According to the United States Department of Health and Human Services, if you get enough sleep, you can reduce your stress levels and be a lot more pleasant in your interaction with the people around you.

Brain Fog

Sleeping well will ensure that you will wake up with a clear mind which will set the tone for the day ahead. You will also improve your concentration skills and be able to focus on any task you set out to do for the day (MyHealthFinder, 2020).

Proposed Sleep Schedule

I felt it was only right to add in a little section about how much sleep people should be getting. How do you know if you are getting enough, too little, or too much sleep? This is a sleep schedule that is based on the recommendation of the Centers for Disease Control and Prevention (CDC).

Newborns

- 0 to 3 months: 14 to 17 hours sleep per day

Infants

- 4 to 12 months: 12 to 16 hours sleep per day

Toddlers

- 1 to 2 years: 11 to 14 hours sleep per day

Preschoolers

- 3 to 5 years: 10 to 13 hours sleep per day

School Going

- 6 to 12 years: 9 to 12 hours sleep per day

Teenagers

- 13 to 18 years: 8 to 10 hours sleep per day

Adults

- 18 to 60 years: 7 plus hours sleep per day

Elderly

- 61 to 64 years: 7 to 9 hours sleep per day

Seniors Citizens

- 65 plus years: 7 to 8 hours sleep per day (CDC, 2017)

Disorders That Interfere With Quality of Sleep

As mentioned at the beginning of this chapter, many people would give anything to get a good night's sleep. Unfortunately, due to any number of conditions, they are not able to get the quality of sleep that is required and needed. In an article written by Danielle Pacheco, and medically reviewed by Dr. Anis Rehman, for the Sleep Foundation, Ms. Pacheco takes a look at some of the sleep disorders that people suffer from. Here is a list of disorders that could prevent you from sleeping the required number of hours per night. This is by no means a complete list of sleep-disrupting disorders, but some of the more well-known ones.

- Insomnia
- Sleep Apnea
- Narcolepsy
- Restless Leg Syndrome
- Sleepwalking
- Night Terrors
- Parasomnias
- Sleep Paralysis
- REM Sleep Behavior Disorder (Pacheco, 2020)

Improving Quality of Sleep

If you are struggling to fall asleep at night, and you do not have any sleep disorders, you might need to tweak your lifestyle. That would mean making some changes that will leave you feeling frustrated. In Chapter 10, we looked at the effect habits have on our daily lives. We also discovered that changes are not as bad as we envision. If you want to improve areas in your life, then you have to start believing that you can do anything you set your mind to.

Consistency

Be consistent with the times you go to bed and wake up. Make sure you have everything you need before you retire for the night such as locking up the house, turning lights out, having your water bottle, and whatever else you need before getting into bed.

Ditch the Screens

The bedroom is not the setting for social gatherings. The bedroom is where you are meant to relax, sleep, and get rest. At least half an hour before going to bed, consider turning all screen devices off, or at least leaving them in another part of the house. Televisions, mobile phones, tablets, and computers are distractions that stimulate the brain when you should be relaxing. Devices emit what is known as blue lights, which are lights made up of electromagnetic radiation. These lights are a type of energy that is invisible to the human eye but does affect the way our brains work by the amount of energy they emit when we are working on our devices. It is for this reason that it is recommended that devices be turned off before going to bed. Many might argue that some settings and apps could be used but the idea of getting the necessary sleep is to eliminate distractions and the temptation to sneak a peek at your social media accounts during the night.

Limit Caffeine and Alcohol

Caffeine and alcohol are stimulants that keep the brain active. Limiting the consumption of alcohol, caffeine, and even large meals before bedtime will allow your body to prepare for a restful night's sleep.

Other Helpful Tips

There are many different tips and tricks to help you get the sleep you need:

- Meditation
- Prayer
- Stop smoking
- Limit day time naps
- Essential oils
- Humidifiers or diffusers

When Sleep Becomes the Center of Your Universe

Until now, we have focused on the benefits of sleep, and looked at why our bodies need sleep. We know how much we should be sleeping according to the recommendations from the CDC. There have even been some sleep training tips to help you unwind and get the quality sleep your body needs to function. In this section, we will take a look at the negative effects of getting too much sleep, backed by an article written for the online blog publication, *Amerisleep* by Rosie Osmun and fact-checked by Michele Roberge. Another negative effect of too much sleep, or more like idolizing sleep, will be explored.

Too Much of a Good Thing Is Not Good

In the previous section, we looked at the benefits of getting sufficient sleep. Many of those benefits are repeated with the opposite effect of getting too much sleep. Without repeating anything, I will give a list of some of the side effects of oversleeping. This list is merely an example, and if you are concerned about your health, consider visiting your doctor for a checkup and diagnosis.

- Depression
- Cognitive impairment
- Degenerative disease
- Chronic inflammation
- Joint and back pain
- Glucose intolerance

When Sleep Becomes an Addiction

This may seem a little surreal to be honest, and you might be wondering how sleep be or become an addiction. The answer would be the same as how smoking, alcohol, prescription medication, illegal drugs, or pornography became additions. Addiction is defined as the act of focusing all your attention on an activity or a substance, as per the Merriam-Webster dictionary.

Is it possible to become addicted to sleeping? I believe it is. When you allow anything to control your life, you are giving that activity or action permission to dictate what you do with your life. The addiction to sleep is real and relevant. I have heard of instances where people cancel prior engagements to stay at home and sleep.

As we have seen in the previous sections, too much sleep, including sleep addiction, could lead to serious health concerns. People who want to spend their time sleeping sometimes make use of sleeping aids such as prescription sleeping tablets or over-the-counter medication to induce drowsiness. Sleep addiction is real, and it can affect your life to the point where it can break your family apart.

Leon shares his experience with sleep addition and the destruction of his home life. He does not want anyone to feel sorry for him, and he is only sharing his story to make people aware of what addiction can do.

I was a contract worker who spent six months of the year on a boat in the Antarctic. Every six months, I would leave my wife and our son at home to earn a supplementary income. In essence, I was earning two salaries and the Antarctic trip was to build up our nest egg for the future. After four successful trips, I returned home and became violently ill. I had developed an infection in my leg which was not healing and I was put off work for six weeks. My wife carried on with her life, going to work and doing what wives do I guess, and I was at home with my young son.

It was also during the convalescence that I started spending a lot more time in my bed, and a lot less time doing much else. I had no reason to be in bed all day long, my infection was healing and all was looking good for me to go back to work. Yet, I could not get enough sleep. I was taking no medication, no substances whatsoever, all I wanted was to stay in bed. I had absolutely no problems sleeping 12 hours a day, going to the bathroom, grabbing something to eat, and heading back to bed to sleep some more.

When it was time to go back to work, I would leave for work as normal but I would be home by midday so that I could go back to bed. This is a pattern that I followed for more than eight months. I was prohibited from going to Antarctica again because I had not been fulfilling my work obligations. I was eventually put on probation and ordered to see a psychiatrist. I was diagnosed with depression, obesity—yes, as short as I am, as round I became—sleep apnea, and type 2 diabetes. According to my doctor, I was a walking timebomb.

I had to make a change. I did not want to use medication because I did not want to become addicted. Oh, the irony. My wife had given up hope that I would ever give up sleeping before my diagnosis, and she started having an affair. I could not really blame her because what I had done was wrong. I put my addiction to sleep above the needs of my wife, my family, and my work. I had created the problem for myself. With help from a counselor, I was able to break my addiction. I was never a religious person. If I was invited to an event at the church, I would find every excuse under the sun not to go, but ironically, to break my addiction to sleep, I turned to God. This passage stood out to me:

"How long will you slumber, O sluggard? When will you rise from your sleep? A little sleep, a little slumber, A little folding of the hands to sleep— So shall your poverty come on you like a prowler, And your need like an armed man," (New King James Bible, 1982, Prov. 6:9-11)

Hearing this verse made me realize that I was doing my family an injustice. I asked for forgiveness and worked hard at turning my life around. Sadly, my marriage ended. My wife did not believe I could change, and instead, she moved on with someone she met at work. I did not blame her, and I could not be angry with her. I was responsible for my actions because I had allowed addiction to rule my life. Where people are addicted to smoking, medication, alcohol, and drugs, I was addicted to sleeping.

In Summary

There is a time and place for everything. Sleep is important to our overall health and well-being, but so is rest. God provides us with just enough, and He knows what is best. As soon as we start believing more, and put more faith in God and what He wants from us, we will struggle to find what we are looking for. I am going to end this chapter with a couple of Bible readings that will hopefully help you understand the balance between necessity and non-essential for self-gain.

And on the seventh day God ended His work which He had done, and He rested on the seventh day from all His work which He had done. Then God blessed the seventh day and sanctified it, because in it He rested from all His work which God had created and made, (New King James Version, 1982, Gen. 2:2-3).

Do not love sleep, lest you come to poverty; Open your eyes, and you will be satisfied with bread, *(New King James Version, 1982, Prov. 20:13).*

In both verses, the message is clear that sleep is necessary, but also not to sleep more than what is necessary. The first verse shows us that after six days of hard work, a day of rest is prescribed by God. The second verse tells us that sleep is a gift, and not to be taken advantage of for selfish reasons.

Chapter 13:

Creating New and Beautiful

Memories

Memories are little treasures that are locked away in trinket boxes. The boxes can be shoeboxes, wooden boxes, or little pockets in your mind. Regardless of the shape of these memory boxes or cases, they are your most treasured possessions going back to your childhood.

Not all the memories in these boxes or cases are good, and often the negative memories come out to plague you when least expected. We do not have a lot of control over the memories in our storage units, and all it takes is a trigger, something familiar, to bring that memory to the foreground.

Since we started this book, we have learned a lot. The journey until now has been interesting, with a lot of discovery about yourself. Whether you are learning new things about yourself, enjoying a refresher of what you might have forgotten, or piling on a layer of what you know with a fresh look at what you originally learned. It does not matter where in your life journey you are; this book is guiding you and giving you a fresh perspective on what should be important from a different angle.

Memories are not something all people can relate to, or are comfortable digging around in. Some people can give you their entire timeline based on their memories—which is really interesting to witness. Other people can relate to the most traumatic memory and as they reach for the memory, they relieve the pain of that specific memory. I am not saying that all memories are bad, sad, traumatic, or happy, but some memories are best left in the memory vault that is hidden behind thick layers of dust and rusted doorways.

Learn From the Past and Build a Brighter Future

In a normal world, I do have a problem with the past. There are times when I have been the victim of the bullying tactics of someone that insists on throwing their version of the "true" memory in my face. The number of times that has happened to me is way too many to count. In a case such as that, I have repeatedly told the person to leave the past in the past. I cannot change what happened, and I cannot be blamed for a memory they have that is actually a lie.

There are instances where memories are pure and beautiful, such as the birth of a child, or a childhood memory of playing on the sandy beach for the first time. Those are memories worth keeping and treasuring in the special memory folder in our hearts and minds. There are memories that you do not want to keep, but for some reason they are sick, and they keep popping up to remind you of whatever it was that happened. And then there are memories we made where our judgment took a leave of absence and left us to fend for ourselves. Those absent judgment memories are the ones that are hanging around to teach us a lesson. We are going to learn from the past, and move forward on our life journey.

As a youngster, I was told by a pastor that when we ask God for forgiveness, He forgives us and the sins we have committed are forgiven. While the past has been deleted by being forgiven, a residual copy is kept by Satan, who will remind us of those trespasses at any time he deems necessary. If you know you have done or said something, and you prayed to God for forgiveness, then you have to know that God has cleaned the slate. God will never remind you of a past wrong.

It Is Your Story

Everyone has a story to tell. In fact, from the moment you are conceived, your story begins. Your parents will start your story until you are old enough to make your own decisions and choices, at which point you become the author of your life story. Your story is unique to you. It will not be perfect, it will have holes, it will have many stops and starts, but the most important thing to remember is that it is a work in progress. There are no do-overs but there are opportunities to correct a mistake from a previous scene. Take that mistake or error in judgment and build it on the foundation of the error to make it bigger, better, and brighter than before. The power is in your hands.

Acknowledge Your Mistakes

This is something that has been mentioned previously. If you have knowingly wronged someone, or done something you are not proud of, be the better person and acknowledge what you have done. By acknowledging your error in judgment, you are showing that you want to move forward and not be kept back. The same can be said for people that intentionally hurt you by using their words, by bullying you because they are unhappy in their own lives, or someone stealing from you and lying about it. Those are pretty unforgivable actions, but be the better person and forgive them. You do not know what tomorrow will bring. For all you know, tomorrow might be that or those persons last day on this earth, and forgiving them will give you the peace you need to carry on living instead of being plagued by conscience. Yes, I realize they hurt you, but by not forgiving the offenders, you will be struck down by a guilty conscience. Be the bigger person, it's not going to cost you anything.

Learn From the Bad Experiences

There is a lesson in every experience you encounter during your journey through life. You may have more negative experiences than good, but you have the power to turn the situation around. When nothing is going right, and you feel like the odds are against you, I always remember the adage, "When life gives you lemons, make lemonade." It reminds me that no matter how bad a situation may seem, there is always a way to find the good.

If you have had a bad experience that has backed you into a corner, stop where you are. Do not panic. Take a couple of deep breaths. Clear your mind. Place yourself on the other side of the situation and think about how you can change the outcome. It is okay if the outcome you settle on is not the one you originally planned on having. There is a life lesson in that outcome. Everything works out the way it is meant to.

No Apology? Move along

If you have been waiting for an apology for six weeks, it is safe to assume that you will never get that apology. Some people have a hard time saying "I'm sorry." Those same people come back six weeks later and act as though they have done nothing, and in fact, they end up playing the victim. This is a real-life scenario where a younger sibling verbally abused her older sibling by saying mean and hurtful things. It is just very unfortunate that on the day the younger sibling started her tirade, is when a family member passed away. The younger sibling was mean and vindictive and chose her words very carefully, leaving her older sibling stunned.

The younger sibling ignored her sister for six weeks. She eventually broke the silence by wishing her older sibling for her birthday, six weeks after the blackout. A week later, the younger sibling sent her sister a message which started with, "I know you are angry with me, but could you lend me money?" And just like that, the older sister had to forget? The older sibling let me know that she forgave her sibling, and she knows she will never get an apology, but she has not forgotten what happened, especially on the day a beloved family member passed away.

It is okay not to get an apology, chances are it will not be sincere if the person is vindictive. From your side, forgive the other person. Forgetting will take time, but it is important that you forgive and do not bring the past up. Leave it in the past.

The Benefits of Beautiful Memories

No matter what you believe about yourself, please know that you should not base your memories on the negative beliefs you have been told or learned throughout your life journey thus far. No matter what you are going through in your life, look for the positives. It might seem impossible, but you have to believe that the positive memories are within your reach. You are not alone, regardless of what you think. At the start of this journey, I promised to be with you every step of the way. I believe I have upheld my promise thus far. Believe in yourself, and believe that your past does not define who you are today.

Focus

Take the time to build memories without depending on technology. Ditch the screens. Take a couple of days a week off social media. Go on a hike, go to the museum, or invite a friend to coffee and make new memories. Reminiscing about old memories with friends or family can help you stay focused on what is important in your life.

No One Can Hack Into Your Brain

What goes on in your brain, only you will know. The memories, stories, and secrets you hold in your memory pockets could make you a wealthy person. When it comes to memories, there will always be three versions—their version, your version, and the version as it occurred. When you depart from this earth one day, no one will be able to take your memories. Life is short, make new memories every day, tell more stories, but leave the secrets. Enough is going on in our lives to hold onto more secrets.

Chapter 14:

Creating Your Tailormade

Lifestyle: One Piece at a Time

Since the start of our journey together, we have explored many different aspects of our lives that we never realized had an impact on who we are or what we are supposed to be. A lot of what you thought were your own goals and aspirations were deeply embedded into your mind from when you were a youngster. Throughout this journey, you have been learning that it is perfectly okay to have an opinion, it is acceptable to have choices, and it is fine if you do not agree with someone else's beliefs. At no point during this journey have you been forced to sign your life away or forced into thinking one way or the other.

It is time to build your tailormade lifestyle based on your own beliefs and what you want for your future. There is nothing to fear as you start searching your soul to find what you have been missing. Uncover some hidden treasures you had stored away, and bring them back to life.

At the start of this journey, you were concerned that you were nothing and that you were not important. I do believe that you have discovered that you are more valued than you believed. The treasures you hold within you are worth more than you will ever know. That is why it is time to incorporate everything you have learned during this journey, and even before, and apply it to your lifestyle, one that will shine brighter than any star in the sky. Open your heart and mind as we look at some tools for you to use to carve your tailormade lifestyle.

Makula Bank of Beliefs

Welcome to the Makula Bank of Beliefs. The terms and conditions for my bank are easy to understand, but not so easy to implement. Each visit will get easier. You may return to my bank at any time of the day or night. You are not limited to the number of visits you make in a day, a week, or a month. The Makula Bank of Beliefs does not discriminate and does not condone any discrimination of any way, shape, or form. There is only one requirement that is asked, and it is that you leave all negativity, self-doubt, and fear in the 10-foot at the front door. Thank you for visiting the Makula Bank of Beliefs.

Recovering Your Lost Beliefs

If you have lost your will to believe, and you do not feel that you are worthy, I am here to tell you that you should not give up. Pick yourself up and start over. Remember, you are the author of your life story, and you have an unlimited amount of stops and starts, but you will need to remember that you will have to settle down and restart your story. If you have lost your way, or believe that your belief system no longer works, let us take a look at how you can find your way back.

Give Yourself a Break

You are and will forever be your harshest critic. Guess what? You are allowed to make mistakes. Mistakes happen! They're how we learn. If you have made a mistake, give yourself a stern talking to, accept that you made a mistake or had an error in judgment, and move forward.

Positivity

Do not be afraid to be grateful for what you have or what you have accomplished. It is hard to be positive when it seems as if the negativity is suffocating you. Do the best you can to remain positive.

Do Not Look Back

A lesson that I learned when I gave my life to God was that you should never carry your old baggage with you. Whatever happened yesterday, last week, last month, or 10 years ago should be laid to rest. Leave your worries, troubles, and uncertainties at the foot of the cross, and walk away. Do not turn back or be tempted to step back into the past.

There Is No Place for Fear

Do not allow fear to hold you hostage. In addition to being your worst critic, you are also your worst enemy. You do not have to be a superhero to conquer your fear. Adopt a lot of faith and belief in yourself, and acknowledge the fear that is gripping you, but do not allow the fear to control your life. You do have the last say.

Believe in Yourself

As we have said multiple times throughout this book, no one can tell you what you should believe in. Your instinct will alert you when you are on the wrong path. Whatever path you choose or end up on, is part of your life lesson. If it does not work out for you, visit the Makula Bank of Beliefs and poke around until you find something that resonates with you. Over time, the belief banks will grow in size as everyone starts depositing their redundant beliefs and withdrawing new ones. Beliefs do not have to be discarded but they can be recycled to fit in with the current climate.

Believe That Your Life Is a Precious Gift

No matter what life throws at you, you are where you need to be. Your life has a purpose, even if you do not see it. Until you start noticing the greatness in yourself, you will never believe that your existence is a precious gift to everyone around you, including yourself. Use your journal or notebook I keep on bringing up. Start a new page titled "Gratitude Yesterday, Today, and Tomorrow" and make a list of everything you have achieved and what you are grateful for each day. Before long, you will believe that your life is a precious gift.

Every Day Is Important

Do not allow yesterday to be a prequel for tomorrow. If yesterday was a bad day where everything imaginable went wrong, know that tomorrow will be better. Yesterday might have left you drained, defeated, and confused, but there was a lesson that needed to be learned. Look for that message, and start a new day tomorrow implementing yesterday's lesson. Yesterday is as important as today, and today is as important as tomorrow. Every day is a new day, and every day is important.

Live Your Life to the Fullest

As much as you liken yourself to a superhero, you will have to admit at some point that you are just a regular human being. You cannot solve the problems of the world. Enjoy the life you have been given. Live today and let tomorrow sort itself out. Honestly, if you are going to spend your time worrying about the past and the future, you are missing the wonderful opportunity of today. Do not be afraid to let your hair or your guard down. You only have one today, so make the most of what you have.

Open Your Heart and Let Love In

This is a difficult one for a lot of people. It is part of our human nature to guard a heart that has been broken, trampled on, or hurt. As a child, you trusted and loved without thinking about it. The older you get, the more you are exposed to, such as the first break up, the loss of someone, or the ultimate betrayal by a close friend. It is time to put a little faith in your judgment, open your heart, and allow for love to envelop you. This is not about dedicating your heart to a forever love, this is about allowing others to show you that they care about you. It is not a sign of weakness to love or be loved.

Soul Searching: Digging Deep to Find Your Purpose in Life

Your tailormade lifestyle is nearing completion, and all that is needed is the glue to put all the pieces together. It might seem pretty straightforward, but you want to find a specific blend of glue that cannot be bought anywhere. You are going to be digging around in all the corners of your conscience, finding what drives you, what keeps you motivated, what inspires you, or what you value above all else. Most of what you are going to be searching through has been hidden by you at some point during your life, but it is time to start digging.

We are building a new and improved you. The foundation is there, it is the structure that needs some work. You did not do anything wrong. Life happens, and we lose track of ourselves. Guess what? It happens to everyone, regardless of how Christian-like, spiritual, good, or bad we are.

Why Should You Search Your Soul?

When you are standing at one of the crossroads life throws at us, we are left to make a choice. This is something we have mentioned often, you need to choose the path. There is no right or wrong path, but keep in mind that each path has its own set of trials and tribulations. It is impossible to see in the future, so we have to choose a path with a positive attitude, believing it is a good one.

When you start feeling that your life does not seem to have a purpose, or if you are unhappy in your current situation, you will know that it is time to start searching deep in your soul. When you start digging around in your conscience, you might not like what you find hidden in there, but use it to your advantage. Recycle the memories that you are uncovering, build them up, and use them to piece your tailormade lifestyle together.

Searching Your Soul

There are no set rules when it comes to soul searching. Everyone has their own ways to dig deep. Soul searching is not meant to be scary, nor is it something dark and evil. As we have mentioned, you will be looking at memories and feelings that have been locked away for a day, three months, or 20 years. You will uncover beliefs you had locked away and habits that. Basically, you are going to go on an expedition to your mind palace.

I will be sharing a couple of examples of the techniques I use when soul searching. These techniques are merely a guide, and you can do whatever you feel comfortable with. As you enter your mind palace, do not be intimidated if you struggle to find your inner self. Have an open mind. Do not dwell on any of the negatives you might encounter. You can use those negatives and shape them into the positives you may need.

Spiritual Meditation

When I meditate, I find a quiet place in my home. I turn on some instrumental Christian music to play in the background. Before I get comfortable, I start with a prayer asking for guidance. Verbalize what you are hoping to find during this expedition. If you are not religious, skip the prayer and start with some deep breaths. Open your heart and find the answers you are looking for.

Alone: You and Your Thoughts

I turn off all distractions, from the radio to the mobile phone. I find a spot in the house where I am feeling comfortable—the setting changes every couple of days. My favorite place to "be one with myself" is on the porch in summer. I pull my journal out and start with a prayer for guidance. I spend at least an hour a week in my mind palace. I analyze my thoughts, document everything, and create a plan of action of what I would like to accomplish. At the end of my digging and poking, I end off with a prayer of thanks.

Adopt a Hobby

Instead of spending 14 hours a day on the computer, either playing *Minecraft* or trolling Facebook, Instagram, YouTube, or Twitter, adopt a hobby. I was addicted to YouTube. I acknowledged it and over a period of three months, I weaned myself off of watching various family vlogging channels. I am not going to lie, I do actively follow three families but from spending six hours a day being one with the families, I am down to 45 minutes a day at the most. To curb my YouTube addiction, I turned to gardening. I have an indoor garden that is made up of two miniature orchids, one regular orchid, and six pot plants. Outside, I have a container garden where I am nursing two miniature apple trees. And then there is my porch, which is my growing space. I am currently growing three plants, and nursing some peppadew seedlings. Gardening has taught me to look deep into my soul to find my nurturing side.

In Summary

Never forget who you are. No matter what you do, always remember that you are on this earth for a reason. If you were not meant to be part of this world, you would not have beaten millions of sperm to fertilize the egg that created you. If ever you find yourself doubting your existence, remember that little tidbit. You are special. You are unique. You are meant to be part of the human race.

You are and always will be important to someone. You hold your future in the palm of your hand, and you get to choose the type of person you want to be. Do not let your past dictate your future and do not allow your past to weigh you down. You cannot change what happened in the past. It is over with. Leave the baggage in the past. If people insist on bringing your past into the present, tell them that you do not need them in your life. Surround yourself with positive people.

Chapter 15:

Creating Your Tailormade

Lifestyle: Putting the Pieces

Together

In Chapter 14, you learned how to revisit your beliefs, recycle old ones, and basically, just an in-depth look at how re-analyzing your core beliefs could be used to create a unique design. I am not going to repeat everything we have already gone through. Each chapter has a little bit of information that can be used to build yourself up and furnish you with all kinds of bold and beautiful traits without compromising who you are.

I showed you how I go soul searching. There are many different ways to connect with your inner self and it is not a one-size-fits-all. I am almost certain you have also been through certain stages in your life where your peers tell you to look into your heart or soul to find what you are looking for. Thinking about this reminded me of a time when a friend of a friend was hoping to get a car after his uncle had passed away. The young lady dealing with the estate of the uncle was told by multiple people that it was his wish for his nephew to have the car. To cut a very long and sad story short, after the promises from the young lady that the nephew would get the car, she changed her mind, did not tell anyone of her plans, and sold the car for her financial gain.

The young lady assured everyone that she had done a lot of soul searching with regards to the car, which was not worth much money and her heart told her that she needed the money more, and that is why she listened to her heart and grabbed the money. The nephew is perfectly happy with the outcome, he insisted from the beginning that he was not at all interested in getting anything from his uncle. Understandably all the friends were very angry, but the nephew said that his soul searching told him to be money-hungry, he was not interested in searching for his uniqueness.

This is an example of what we do not want from soul searching, nor from reshaping our beliefs. Putting money as the focus point is wrong, and is a sign of greed. This chapter is going to be focusing on all the positive ways of using the glue we mentioned in the previous chapter. We are going to learn how to apply our beliefs, find our strengths and weaknesses and create our unique, tailormade lifestyle that will be balanced. In other words, your very own, perfectly personal balanced lifestyle.

Applying Your Beliefs

Chapter 2 and Chapter 3 are dedicated to all things based on beliefs, from belief systems and what people believe in analyzing beliefs and where beliefs originated from. Throughout the whole book, I have brought up little hidden messages about believing in a higher power, namely God. If you are not a religious person, you are encouraged to believe in yourself, and your ability to be the best you can be. Not once were you bullied, nor were you forced to do something you were not ready for. Okay, I admit, I did kind of insist that you get yourself a journal, but that was the only bit of persuasion I came up with, and I was nice about it.

Chapter 3 is based on analyzing beliefs, as well as core beliefs, and where beliefs originated from. In the interest of not repeating everything already mentioned, I am going to build on from what was previously discussed, and add it to building a new lifestyle. Your new lifestyle is going to be one that has no specific order as you will be creating your own belief system. Your beliefs will no longer be dictating your life, nor will they be holding you hostage.

Beliefs Refresher

As previously mentioned, your belief system helps you cope with difficult and stressful situations that accompany everyday life. No matter who you believe in or do not believe in, you have someone or something to put your belief in. It is time to start shifting your focus a little bit. No, I am still not going to force you to believe in something or someone you are not ready to. I would like you to start getting used to the idea of believing in yourself.

Beliefs are categorized based on various sources. It is up to us, as individuals, to make a decision based on what we believe. Your belief is yours, and we have said that many times throughout this book and it will probably be mentioned a couple more times before we reach the final destination. This is your journey and I am your guide.

- Evidence

- Tradition

- Authority

- Association by influence

- Belief by revelation

It is important to remember that nobody can tell you want to believe in. You were told to challenge your beliefs based on the categories and to put your beliefs to the test. Research, lots of research got you to the place where you were able to form your own beliefs. You have now reached the stage where you are getting ready to apply your beliefs after digging deep into your soul to find the answers and peace you were looking for.

Analysis and Application of Beliefs

Throughout this book, we have been changing certain aspects of our core beliefs. We cleaned our glasses, wiped our screens to get a clearer look at what we were faced with. As we are entering the final stages of the journey, we are very close to creating a lifestyle that is ours alone, individually designed for with your beliefs riding shotgun. It really does not get any better than that.

Advantages and Disadvantages

Compare and weigh the advantages and disadvantages of your beliefs.

Time Projection

Envision what your new or recycled beliefs will be like in the future.

Beliefs Are All Over

Challenge your beliefs and take note of where and how they shape your life.

Social Networking

Join social media groups that fall under the same category as your beliefs.

This is a very limited list of beliefs and how to apply them to your life. If you go back to Chapter 3, you will find more examples. Do not be afraid to explore, analyze and apply your beliefs to a system that works for you.

Strengths and Weaknesses of Belief

Before you can put the pieces of your new, tailormade lifestyle, based on beliefs, together, we are going to look at a list of strengths and weaknesses. You are going to have to separate your strengths from your weaknesses so that you can see which of the areas of your belief systems need more building. I do believe that this is an exercise that should happen frequently. You should keep up with the current trends, and not have to undo all the hard work you have done to get to this point.

Signs That You Are Strong In Your Beliefs

Kindness

People tend to view kindness in people as a sign of weakness. This is because kind people have compassion for others, and take the time to listen and help if and when needed.

Acknowledgment of Weakness

Many people see an acknowledgment as a declaration of stepping down or backing away, admitting that they are not as strong as what they would like people to believe. Shusaku Endo stated, "Every weakness contains within itself a strength." This quote will set the naysayers straight.

Patience

Having patience in any situation is a sign of strength. I have often seen people lose their tempers because they have to wait their turn in the checkout queue. Or seeing someone keeping to the speed limit on the road and the person behind them is furiously honking their horn to get them to speed up. Many will view being patient as a sign of weakness or giving in to a situation, but to practice patience shows that you are calm under pressure and can diffuse a volatile situation without reacting in anger or frustration.

Reaching Out for Help

Reaching out or admitting someone needs help is not a sign of weakness as any would like to believe. Asking for help is one of the most courageous things I have seen.

Failure

In the same vein as reaching out, admitting that you cannot do something is not a sign of weakness. It takes a person of strength and courage to admit when they cannot reach the point to complete something they started out doing.

Signs That You Are Weak In Your Beliefs

No Motivation

If you keep telling yourself that you cannot do something, or that you are not worthy of something, then you are telling your peers that you are weak in your character. Of course, you will balk at the phrase of being weak, but in reality, if you do not have the motivation you are seen as a weakling.

Little to No Self-Control

My Mom, along with everyone else's moms, loved to say, "If you can't say anything nice, don't say anything at all." I also remember my mother's version being accompanied by a cuff on the ear. If you cannot put a filter before your mouth, or refrain from over-indulgence indicating that you have no willpower which is a sign of weakness.

Self-Centered

If you walk around believing the world and its followers owe you for being part of the existence, you are placing yourself on a pedestal. As you may know, pedestals have no place in our lives, as we should all be treated equally.

If you are judging someone based on something you too are guilty of, you are just as weak as your judgment. Refer to Matthew 7:1-5 in your Bible, or go back to Chapter 4, under the subtitle "What Is Religion."

Creating a Balanced Lifestyle

There are no rules about how to balance life, much less create a lifestyle. This is a topic only the person setting off on the adventure can create. Oh, I can give you tips and I can guide you, but creating the balance you crave for your life is in your hands. I can tell you that creating and maintaining a balance in your life is essential for your overall health and wellbeing.

To create a balanced life is going to take a bit of homework on your part. Armed with your notebook or journal, write down areas of your life where you believe balance would be beneficial. Once you have completed your list, you can use the balance beam to restructure your lifestyle to be more effective.

Structure of Balance

Assessing Your Current Way of Life

If you are spending more time at work, out with friends, or putting the needs of others ahead of your own happiness and personal relationships, you have fallen off the balance beam. You need to stop what you are doing, take a step back, and prioritize what is important to you. We know that having work and money is important to our existence, but at what cost does it have to come to you? Be kind to yourself, after all, you are only human. You are one person trying to do the tasks of 10. It is okay to have priorities where you are first, second, third, and fourth on the list.

Making a Decision and Sticking to It

This one pretty much aligns with the way you assess your way of life. I have already given you permission to have priorities, and this only doubles up as a not-so-subtle reminder that you can do whatever you want to, to ensure your for today, tomorrow, and the future.

Schedules

Keep a schedule. Not only does a schedule remind you where and when events are happening, but it is also a way to keep you grounded. In addition to your journal, it might just be time to bring in a new friend—a daily planner. Ensure that everyone has access to your planner so that they too, can hold you accountable and remind you that you need to maintain balance.

Goal-Setting

This is one we dealt with in Chapter 1 and it was touched on multiple times. Having a list of goals, reasonable ones, are the backbone of maintaining a healthy balance in your life. If you are struggling to find balance in any area of your life, look at your list of goals. You should have many of those goal lists in your notebook by now.

Take Risks

Part of a healthy balance in your life is also living on the edge. Do not be afraid to step outside of your comfort zone. If you have never gone fishing, be a rebel and head out to the local river and try it. You might find that you will "be one with nature," and even if you do not catch anything, you will know that you did something you never thought you would do. Let me be clear about something, taking risks is not a green light for you to do something irresponsible, such as invest your salary in a Ponzi scheme. Responsible risk-takers are those who know right from wrong but veer off the path to venture into the unknown without causing or inflicting harm.

Chapter 16:

Building the Bridge: Crossing It

With Self-Confidence

At this stage of the book, you are most probably hyperventilating at the thought of venturing out into this crazy world, filled with doom and gloom, entitled Karen's who believe they are right and that everyone owes them, controversy. Truth be told, my anxiety levels would be through the roof too, except they are not. I am as cool as a cucumber, knowing that the choices I make in my life were made with confidence. If you do not have confidence in yourself, you are going to crumble into dust.

If you have learned anything until now, it is that you are capable of greatness. You need to believe in yourself and believe that you can do anything you set your mind to. Like many other billions of people, you too have been bullied, have had your peers or mentors belittle you and tell you that you would amount to nothing, or simply just believed that you were worthless. Today, right now, I am going to tell you that you need to buck up and face your fears.

With everything that is going on in the world, you need to step up, find your spot and assert yourself. You are not going to fade away into the background or fly under the radar. You need to *believe* in *yourself*. I want you to succeed and I want you to use your talents and uniqueness to inspire and touch the hearts and lives of others. Every single person on this planet and I will even throw in the animal kingdom, is confident. It is just that some people have forgotten where they put theirs. Let us go on a journey together to find your confidence so that you can believe in yourself again. Grab your journal—you can leave the planner behind for now—and let's get going.

While this chapter is all about finding and restoring your self-confidence and boosting your beliefs, a warning is called for. Enjoy the newfound self-confidence you uncovered but do not be too over-confident. Too much of a good thing is not always good, and quite frankly, being over-confident could potentially lead to disappointment and failure.

Confidence and Belief: The Hunt Begins

Yes, this section is meant to indicate that we mean business. There is no more pussyfooting around, and no more avoidance. What happened yesterday is over and forgotten. If you could not fry an egg yesterday, you will learn to fry one today or tomorrow. There are many different tools to help you gain confidence, as well as helping you believe in yourself. I will guide you through a handful of the tips and tools, and I will leave you with a list you can explore on your own. Okay, deep breath in through the nose, and slowly exhale through the mouth. Keep an open mind, and be ready to see changes.

Switching Negativity With Positivity

Make a list of all the negative aspects you consider to form part of your life. Once you have made your negative list, replace the negative with positives. For each of the new positive entries on your list, write an affirmation. It could look something like this:

- Negative: Nothing is going according to plan.

- Positive: Everything will work out as it should.

- Affirmation: I believe that everything will be okay.

Your lists will take on any form, as there are no set guidelines. The most important takeaway here is that you deal with all your negative beliefs about yourself, the people around you, and life. You do not want to go through life surrounded by a murky cloud of negativity.

Overcome Biggest Fears

Okay, do not skip this one because you are not ready to face a fear that has been crippling you for longer than you know. For all you know, that fear might not even be as daunting now as it was when you developed it. Write down your fear. It is not going to jump up off the page and attack you. Acknowledge that you have a fear, and express how it makes you feel. What you are doing here is believing in yourself by acknowledging that you have a fear. You are going to be confident and release the fear.

Pay Attention to the Solution, Not the Problem

My laptop decided it was going to give me the blue screen of death. Instead of taking a deep breath and calming myself before panicking, I missed steps one, two and three, and dove straight into the flaming hot pool of lava. First and foremost, in my mind was that all the work I had done was gone, sucked in cyber oblivion, and gone forever. Eight hours' worth of work that I would normally have saved and backed up at regular intervals, but well, Microsoft Word being what it is, it decided not to play nicely. There I was, panicking, frustrated, and angry at the laptop for blue screening me, when I should have been looking at it from a different perspective.

So, I did not save my work—that was on me. I had thankfully uploaded most of the work onto my external drive, so that was good. I looked at the situation as an outsider and realized, this was God's way of telling me I needed a break from the laptop. When God gives me signs, I listen. After two hours away from my laptop, I started it up again. I was calmer and thinking more clearly. All that was needed was a level heard and not being like a bull that sees red.

Other Self-Help Tips

- Make a list of past and present successes.

- Give the people in your circle the task of working on a list of five positive traits about you.

- Do not view changes as the enemy, embrace them.

- Build on the skills you want to change.

- Instead of complaining, start praising yourself and people, even strangers, around you.

- Acceptance is the key to self-confidence. Knowing you cannot control everything and that by accepting whatever you are going through, you are showing how confident you are.

- If social media influences your life, consider taking a social media break. Social media is not a healthy platform for people suffering from negative self-confidence.

- Consider giving up addictions such as alcohol, drugs, smoking, shopping, pornography, or gambling. This is a list that can go on. Anything that has power over you, is an addiction that should be culled from your life.

Having the Confidence to Make Choices That Benefit Your Beliefs

The question is: *How do you, or anyone else for that matter, know that the choices being made are the right ones?*

The answer is: *You will not know until you make those choices and experience them for yourself.*

This section is going to be looking at your decision-making choices. We are our own worst enemies at the best of times. We second guess our choices because we are not overly confident. You could almost argue that we are cautiously optimistic.

When making choices or decisions, you need to have an open mind and believe in yourself. This is the whole self-confidence business where you want to build yourself up and focus on the positives and believe that everything is good and well in your Youville. You want to enter any situation with confidence because you know what you are capable of.

You should also realize that when making choices or decisions, there are no right or wrong answers. I can give you some guidelines that you can use to grow, but at the end of the day, you are the only one that will know whether you are on the right track or veering off the path into the unknown. Making choices happens on a trial and error, first come first served, scenario.

No Doubts

If you are confident with the choice you made, then you have to believe in yourself. The moment you "umm" and "ahh" because you are second-guessing a choice, then you do not believe in your choice and the doubt will consume you.

At Peace With Your Choice

Confidence is all about having peace deep within the trenches of your heart. Making choices is about you, who you are, and what you hold dear. The people around you are allowed to have opinions, but ultimately, you hold the cards when it comes to choices. Believe that the choice you are making is the right one.

The Necessity of Choices

There are times when you are forced to make choices. Sometimes the choices are life-altering and no matter how you despise making choices or being put on the spot, a choice has to be made. Choose the option that you feel confident in. If you are struggling to find your confidence, do some soul searching.

The More You Choose, the More Choices Are Made

The reality is, the more confident you become at making the choices without second-guessing yourself, the more choices you will be making. Your confidence will grow and you will be able to act faster, should the need arise.

Having the Confidence to Bounce Back From Misguided Choices

When making choices, always remember that you have options. When I hear people are being negative and they seem unhappy with their lives, I tell them that they have choices and that each choice has options, and those options each have options, and so forth. The choices, whether right or wrong, good or bad, have consequences.

You need to believe in yourself when choosing an option. Listen to your inner voice, that little voice that is always trying to be the voice of reason. You can ignore that voice, and choose whatever is behind door number two, but remember that you might not have the desired outcome.

It is easy to be fooled, and there are times when your confidence becomes a little too blasé. That is when you start making the wrong choices. When making bad choices, you have to take into account that you will face repercussions. More often than not, you can bounce back from bad choices or decisions. Other times, the recovery is going to take a little more time depending on the severity of the choice you made. I know that this sounds disheartening, but it is part of life's precious lessons. It is for this reason that you are cautioned to think before acting and separate your wants from your needs.

Let us take a look at how bad decisions are made. Of course, this is not an open-ended invitation to mimic the author. This is merely a guide to show you how bad choices could be made. I am hoping that by presenting you with this list, you can avoid the traps as they appear.

Emotional

Many choices and decisions are based on emotions. I know that it is easier said than done, but try not to make important choices when emotional. If it is something that needs an immediate and urgent response, consider taking a trusted friend or family member to act on your behalf. Emotions can be any factor that could cloud your judgment such as being sad, frustrated, dismissive, angry, or overly happy.

Fact Check

Making a choice before verifying the facts is never a good idea. A lot of people act on impulse, jump in with both feet, and then start asking questions. The right thing to do is to do your research, ask around, research a little more, and then either commit or walk away. Remember, if something sounds too good to be true, you are making a good choice by researching.

Listen to Your Inner Voice

Your inner voice or gut is not trying to deceive you or prevent you from having fun. That voice you hear when doing something you know you probably should not be doing, you know, the voice that almost sounds like your mother's voice. Yes, that one. Do yourself a favor—listen to it! If you are faced with a choice, and you know it is something you desperately want but there is something that is telling you to walk away, rather walk away. For all you know, tomorrow may just bring a better opportunity.

Chapter 17:

Life Lessons: Learning From

Mistakes

When I started thinking about writing a book about beliefs, I had intended it to be about me. Almost like a journal or daily devotion pocket guide. I was like billions of people in this world that did not believe I had it in me to write a book and bare my soul. As I sat down to plan the outline, I found myself hungry for more. I told some friends, who shared it with their friends, and it was not long before I had two pages of contact details for people wanting to share their stories or testimonies. I did have two or three people who told me I was crazy and that they would have no part in anything being spoken about in this book. I respected their wishes. I am a man of my word and honor. I have morals which I will not compromise for anyone.

I think a lot of people were afraid that this book was going to be mostly about religion, but if you have made it this far, you will agree that this book is more information-based than religion-based. We worked together to peel away at the layers you had piled on over the years. Layers, we can agree, were put there to safeguard you from being bullied, abused, or judged by people who took pleasure in making you uncomfortable. Everyone has been in a position like that, but not everyone has the courage to step out of the shadows. Some hurt a little more than others. Some are unsure of this new lifestyle that includes a lot of freedom. Some do not trust anything that they have been learning.

I cannot force anyone to believe in anything they do not want to, whether it is about the people around them, or themselves. Everyone needs to discover who they are in their own time. Until they are ready to make that final leap, I will continue sharing information and real-life stories gathered from people from all walks of life.

The No Judgment Policy

This policy belongs to the Makula Bank of Beliefs. This is a policy that gives everyone who has struggled, is struggling, and will struggle to find themselves, a reprieve. This is something I believe in with every fiber of my existence. I want everyone to learn and accept that judging another person for his actions, appearance, skin color, sexual orientation, or whatever negative thoughts they conjure up, is not okay. We, you and me, and the entire human race do not have the right to tell anyone what they should be doing with their life. We cannot be telling people how to live their lives because we were not asked for our opinions.

In keeping with the No Judgment Policy, I want you to understand that you have a choice. Everyone on this earth has a choice. If you want to walk around being negative, you have to realize what you are doing to everyone you come across, passersby, friends, or family. A little helpful hint that I can give you going forward, is that you keep your attitude in check. Remember this, negativity feeds on itself. Take a couple of moments to reflect on that phrase while I tell you about a lady named Paula, age 65.

Paula is known in her community as someone who thrives on spreading messages of hate while preaching in the same voice. Many people have tried to talk to her about her blasphemous ways and to get her to keep her opinions to herself instead of sharing her hateful messages with the community groups. It has gotten so bad that she has recruited an 86-year-old lady named Gloria to join her pact. Between the two of them spreading hate, anger, and negativity, they have managed to divide a community that once stood together in times of need. Now, unfortunately, it is every person for themselves.

Now that you have had a minute to reflect, can you understand why I feel so strongly about judging people? I have an overwhelming urge to reach out and pull every person who has been branded by the antagonistic ideology of vindictive people who have taken a wrong turn in their lives and are struggling to find their way back. These people, Gloria, Paula, and the likes of them, should be held accountable for their actions but it is not up to you, or me, or my neighbor. It is up to God to pass His judgment when the time is right.

Life Lessons: Understanding the Different Types of Mistakes

I always thought that mistakes were either accidental or intentional, but boy was I wrong. I stumbled across an article titled "5 Types of Mistakes That Can Transform Your Life" written by Nathan Burriston for the online publication *Medium*. I have to give Nathan credit for this interesting article to help us understand the types of mistakes and how they could potentially benefit us. These mistakes fall into the category of life lessons to be learned.

Mistakes by Other People

Life lesson number one, learning by listening to the tales told by others, as well as observing interactions between people. Since the beginning of time—when we were children—we have observed the actions of other children and adults. Growing up, we would store these observations in our memory banks and as life threw us some curveballs, we would recall what we had learned to prevent us from making the same mistakes.

Standard Mistakes

If you make a mistake once, you learn from it and try your utmost never to repeat the mistake a second time. We all make basic mistakes. Imagine running through the meadow, barefoot and without a care in the world. We run through a bed of thorns. Once we deal with those thorns, we navigate our path to avoid the thorns. It will happen more than once, and that is fine because we are learning as we go.

Silly Mistakes

Silly mistakes are not intentional but occur by accident. Say for instance that you are walking down the passage, you lose your footing, collide with the wall, and the mirror decides that today is the day it is going to come crashing down. Glass shards fly all over and seven years of bad luck is imminent. You did not intentionally lose your footing, so it was a silly or clumsy mistake. These mistakes happen frequently, and most of the time we can look back and laugh at how bizarre they were. They do remind you that no one is perfect and accidents happen.

Warning Mistakes

Warning mistakes happen more frequently than what is necessary. They are absent-minded, intentional mistakes that could potentially alter the course of your life. Warning mistakes could potentially lead to tragedies. I believe that these warning mistakes should fall under the standard mistakes category because no one would want to repeat them for fear of a potentially serious or tragic outcome.

Necessary Mistakes

Sometimes we need to make mistakes. We cannot go through life wrapped in cotton wool. The only way we can gain valuable life lessons and experience is by figuring things out for ourselves.

Annabel spent six years of her life with Ryan. They met online when Annabel was 15 years old. Both families were happy for them and they spent weekends and holidays going from one family home to the next.

About two years into the relationship, Annabel's sister and mother started seeing things that concerned them. Annabel started self-harming. No amount of begging and pleading with Annabel helped. Ultimatums did not work, and Annabel started drifting away from her family. After speaking to a counselor who dealt with abusive relationships, Annabel's mother and sister stopped trying to tell her what to do, and instead started praying. After what seemed like an eternity of prayer, the relationship ended. The stories of physical, mental, and verbal abuse left everyone speechless. At the end of six years, this was a necessary mistake that needed to be played out so that it would not be made again.

Mistakes in Summary

Life lessons are not meant to be a walk in the park. We get to make mistakes accidentally because they teach us valuable lessons about ourselves and our characters. While it is human nature to make mistakes, it is not an open invitation to actually go out and make mistakes intentionally. We cannot make it a habit to keep making mistakes hoping to learn a valuable lesson, as some mistakes are hard to reverse due to consequences such as a relationship ending or ending up in prison (Burriston, 2020).

Life Lessons: Do Not Let Fear Hold You Back

"Never let the fear of striking out get in your way."

– Babe Ruth

If you have been knocked down, pick yourself up, dust yourself off, and try again. If you keep telling yourself that you cannot do something or that you are a failure, you will start believing your negative thoughts. Condemn those thoughts, and turn the situation around.

You know that I am all about positivity, and that is what this book has been about. I have wanted to uplift your spirit so that you could see that you are important to this world and to people like me, a stranger. How are you important to me? Pretty easy actually. Knowing that you are reading this book, and knowing that I have filled it with positive tools and tips, allows me to believe that you are learning and that what you are learning will be shared with others.

Do not be afraid to wear your heart on your sleeve. Do not be afraid to make mistakes. Do not be afraid to put yourself out in the world. I am going to leave you with some positive affirmations that you can tell yourself over and over until you believe them and yourself. Feel free to create your own list, and add to it whenever you think of something. Be who you were meant to be, and do not allow failures or errors in judgment to hold you back. Honestly, you are destined for greatness. Love yourself. Believe in yourself. Have faith in yourself.

Positive Affirmations

- I am honest with myself and those around me.
- I have faith that everything will be okay.
- I have faults and that is perfectly okay.
- My past does not define my future.
- I am destined for greatness.
- I have respect for everyone, regardless of who they are or where they come from.
- Tomorrow is another day.
- My success is not measured by the size of my bank balance.
- I have enough faith in myself to carry those who are struggling.
- I believe in the power of prayer.
- I am unique, there is no one else exactly like me.
- I love all my imperfections; they are perfect.
- Giving up is not a choice, it is an option.
- I can do anything I put my mind to.

- I am gorgeous/handsome.
- God never gives me anything I cannot deal with.
- I love the life I had because I know I am being true to my nature.
- I do not pretend to be someone I am not.
- I choose to smile every day.
- I choose to help the people that choose to ignore my existence.

Chapter 18:

Trust Yourself by Being Brave, Wise, and the Person You Want to Be

It is a lovely sunny day, and instead of having lunch indoors, you pack your lunch bag and head out to the park. You find a spot where you can see the landscape before you. Children are playing on the playground. You smile to yourself as you unwrap your turkey, cheese, and mayo sandwich, "this is perfect" you think. As you take the first bite of your sandwich, you notice a little boy standing on his own, away from the group of children on the playground. Why is he standing alone? Is he shy? Why are the other children not inviting him to play with them? Is he perhaps afraid of not fitting in with the group of children? Where are his parents or caregivers? I have all these questions, but no answers.

No matter where in the world, country, state, town, or neighborhood you are in, you will always see or hear of a similar scenario. As has been hinted at over the last couple of chapters, our journey together is nearing its end. We have two more stops after this one until we part ways. As much as I am dreading letting you go out on your own, I realize that it is something I need to come to terms with. It is in my nature to want to protect people, no matter who they are, from the big, crazy, scary world.

Trust

Like the little boy at the playground, you too were an observer before you started searching yourself. You were neither alone nor shy. You were on a quest to understand what you mean to the world and the people in it. Fear once gripped you because you thought you were isolated, and what you believed to be the truth, has been smashed to pieces and ground to dust.

You have been equipped with an arsenal of weapons and tools as we approach the crossroad at the end of our life journey together. For one of us, the road will end but for the other, a brand new adventure awaits. I am confident that you will be a remarkable recruiter because you are a powerful human being.

Be Who You Need to Be—Yourself

Do not let fear hold you hostage. Do not allow the words of anger, hate, and condemnation to rock your world. You have come this far by believing in yourself. You have learned to trust yourself. It is because of you that have gotten here, moments away from starting a new adventure. Trust in yourself with every fiber of your being and believe that you can accomplish anything you set your mind to. The fear that once cloaked and hid you from yourself has been flushed out. You are now swaddled in positivity, and you are ready to embrace your new goals and aspirations.

Setting and Keeping Goals

As discussed in Chapter 10, goals are important to keep you on the straight and narrow, as well as to give you something to look forward to. Continue making your goals, and make them achievable so that you do not lose interest or give up hope. Ensure that you give yourself some leeway to avoid becoming frustrated and losing faith and trust in yourself. Always remember, you are not in a race to see who can get to the finish first. You are building a trust, faith, and belief-based foundation to share with others.

Kindness and Strength

If I have not already told you, or if you have forgotten, you are human and you have feelings. You are your worst enemy and your harshest critic. Turn the sentence into a positive; I am my best friend, and I am the kindest supporter of myself. Love yourself, be kind to yourself, and treat yourself with the respect you command. Be strong, courageous, and brave to make the changes you want to see.

Bravery

Having the courage to step outside your comfort zone is one of the greatest feats you will face. Having confidence fills you with the courage you need to stand up and fight for what is right, and what you believe in. I think it is easier to be brave as a child than courageous as an adult.

As children, we believe everything we are told, to the point that we are gullible. The reason for this is that we trust our peers. The annual dentist visit or the wellness check is a perfect example because children never know what to expect. Mom and Dad will reassure the children by telling them to be brave and if they need a shot or have to have a filling done, that it will not hurt. We march into the dental surgery, chest out, head held high and brave as a bear for what is to come.

As adults, well, we have had time to figure out the truth and know where we stand on the brave bus. It is not as easy to be brave when you have gone through trauma and lose that brave button, along with the malfunctioning trust button. As hard as it might be to be courageous and regain the levels of trust needed, it is something that is vitally important to our existence.

Facing Our Fears

"You gain strength, courage, and confidence by every experience in which you really stop to look fear in the face. You are able to say to yourself, 'I have lived through this horror. I can take the next thing that comes along.' You must do the thing you think you cannot do."

—Eleanor Roosevelt

Living in fear has got to be one of the loneliest experiences anyone can ever go through. I have heard of people being afraid to sleep at night because a noise on the property could potentially mean a home invasion, or some people are deathly afraid of the darkness and will not go to sleep during a power outage. These are real stories and not just made up for content or fluff.

One of the ladies I spoke to, who lives in South Africa, told me about the power problems that her country is facing. In an attempt to generate enough power to keep the lights on across the country, they have what is called "loadshedding," whereby each city is broken down into blocks and assigned a time when their power will be turned off for between two and four hours two to three times a day. When the power goes off in the middle of the night, she will stay awake, regardless of how exhausted she is, because the eerie silence of the darkness scares her.

She has admitted that she has become more confident at facing this demon and for her, it was all about prayer and having faith. Although she still does not go to sleep when the power is off, she is no longer afraid and the sounds she hears do not bother her. She has come to enjoy the middle of the night blackouts because then she can do some work without the distraction of her phone receiving messages, or the temptations of visiting Instagram or YouTube since there is no Wi-Fi during the blackout.

Stand Up for What You Believe In

Bravery is not about being broken or defeated; it is about standing up for what you believe in. Bravery is not about having a physical fight; it is about standing your ground for the sake of your beliefs. Everyone should have the courage to share their views and opinions. Not everyone has to agree with your assessment, nor do you have to agree with what someone else is saying.

I have found that people who are insecure are the ones that attack the hardest. They believe that they are strong and courageous, when in fact they are hiding behind false claims. They plan their attack with the utmost precision, down to the smallest details. The information that they have gathered is almost alarmingly accurate, yet with massive gaps—say 10 years' worth of gaps. The person being attacked has been waiting, so is ready as the punches start. The blows keep coming. The attacker is getting angrier and the insults keep on. The other person is not backing down and counteracts each blow with a truth bomb.

The attacker walks away, angry and frustrated because they believe they were right. The person being attacked showed immense bravery by standing up for what they believed in. Yes, they were deeply wounded by the angry slurs, mean comments, and hate speech that accompanied each blow, but they never once backed away.

Be Who You Are Meant to Be

Why do people pretend to be someone they are not? What is with the nose in the air business and the carrot up the you-know-where? I believe that if you are pretending to be someone else, then you have little to no confidence or self-respect for yourself. As a very open and transparent person, I cannot go around pretending to be something I am not. I am not perfect, I have had my ups and downs, but I am proud of the person I have become.

Besides, I do not need anyone's approval, and neither do you. In God's eyes, we are perfect because we were created in His perfect image. If I were to go out drinking, smoking, gambling, and involved in debauchery every night, I would be showing God that I am not happy with who I am. Ultimately, it would be a sign that I am ungrateful for all the wonderful opportunities He has given me. I am proud of the person I am today and I do not have any desire to be anyone other than myself.

We are going to take a look at a couple of signs to help you become the person you are meant to be.

Priorities Change

A nice positive start is realizing that your goals are changing. You are ready to be responsible and take responsibility for your choices. As you find your feet and realize your self-worth, you start participating in things that are meaningful to you. Many will try to come between you and your new priorities. Some will include your friends and family, and some will be about you and what you want. You do not have to feel guilty or the decisions you make. Be the person you are meant to be.

Dealing With Issues

Being who you are meant to be, starts with dealing with the baggage. Goodness, baggage can weigh anyone down. I often wonder why we do not unpack our baggage in a timely manner, rather than wait for the volcanoes to erupt and the earthquakes to rock the state. Slightly melodramatic, but that is what it is like for a lot of people. We hold onto our issues, and there will be a day that the issue basket in us starts overflowing. Acknowledge the troubles you are having, own them, and leave them in the past. You can do it; I know you can.

Cut the Negative Out of Your Life

This is a bit of a tender point for a lot of people. It is easier to say it than do it. Do we need to ditch the negative people in our lives? What happens if those negative people are part of your family? Yes, this is a difficult one to answer but you have to do what is right for you. I have personally struggled with this one before, and I went for five months without speaking to a family member. I told them the reason, I even gave them an opportunity to change their attitudes, but they were not interested. It is hard for a negative person to see the world in color or see the good in everything. A lot of prayers went into this family member and they called me up after five months of no contact and thanked me for teaching them about being confident, strong, and positive.

Not everyone will have a happy outcome, it depends on the person and how far along they have come in their own life journey. Do not change who you are for anyone. You are where you are meant to be.

The End Is Within Reach

Throughout this journey, I have been with you, at your side or in the palm of your hand. I have encouraged you, filling you with positivity, never once leaving you to figure things out for yourself. I introduced you to yourself, the one you had hidden in a shell deep within your soul. I showed you that you do not have to be stuck in a cage or a display cabinet. You learned to break down your beliefs, analyze your habits, and reinvent who and what you believe in.

This has been an interesting journey, figuring out your importance, self-worth, and realizing that you are more confident than what you ever believed. I have said it many times during this journey, if you do not believe in any specific religion, believe in yourself and know that you are capable of achieving greatness. You are *strong*. You are *brave*. You are *wise*. You are *you*.

Chapter 19:

You Are Unique: Accept and

Embrace Who You Are

I do not know how many more ways I can emphasize how unbelievably special you are. I want you to see in yourself what you are too afraid to see. This is why I love the mirror. Mirrors do not lie. If you want honesty, stand in front of the mirror and take a long look at yourself. Shake the negative thoughts and comments out of your head. You do not need them anymore. Nothing and no one has the right to control you other than you, yourself.

Chapters 1 through 18 have been filled with all things positive. Not once were you judged about the way you have been living your life, not once were you bullied for the choices you made, your appearance, or your lifestyle. If you are holding onto negative thoughts, please get rid of them. Your negative thoughts are holding you hostage. Allow me to be frank with you. Right now, in our present-day and age, we are living in trying times. It is no secret. Whether the end is near or not should not be in the way of our today.

Today is all about you, and honoring you for the unique person you are. Remove the blinkers from your eyes, and shake the negative thoughts and energy from your mind. Create a compartment in your mind where you can see your incredible personality and your individuality and know that there is only one person like you walking around on this earth—*you*!

Importance of Self-Awareness

Who is more qualified to understand you than you, yourself? You know you are special and unique, and not only because I have been telling you. Regardless of what you did in the past, you have learned that you cannot change what happened but you can shape tomorrow. I know that you recognize yourself as being one of a kind, and you are aware of your strength, courage, and weaknesses.

Being aware of your traits is not bad, it is actually excellent because you know where you need a little more improvement or where you need to stand down. Guess what? You are a human being who will make mistakes, have errors in judgment, and you absolutely will miss the bus a couple of times, but all that does is make you even more unique. You have all the tools to pick yourself up and patch up what needs fixing before moving onto something else. Do not be afraid to let your guard down every once in a while.

Benefits of Self-Awareness

I keep on telling you how important it is to be self-aware, and you are agreeing but what you really want to know is, what are the benefits of falling flat on your face in a crowded room? How is your humility benefitting anyone other than being the laughing stock of the room? Firstly, before we hop on over to the benefits, I am going to leave a list of identifiable self-awareness traits that you may or may not possess. The list may or may not have been featured, if not mentioned, in previous chapters.

- Remaining calm in a difficult situation.

- Keeping your emotions under control and looking at the situation from all angles.

- Keeping in mind that you are not meant to fix every situation, and sometimes kindness and compassion are all that is needed without giving solutions.

- Knowing and understanding that there are no perfect human beings, yourself included.

- Acknowledging and owning your mistakes.

- Being true to who and what you are at all times, never being someone or something you are not for the sake of compromising your beliefs and morals.

Okay, now that the scene has been set, and you know without a shadow of a doubt that you acknowledge at least five traits mentioned in yourself, you are ready to look at some of the benefits of self-awareness in any situation.

Good Listeners

In a world where technology is the beginning and end of everything, people do not have one on one conversations anymore. Everything either via text messages, voice messages, or emails. If you know a friend needs your undivided attention, where they can talk without interruptions, you are the person for the task.

Making Good Decisions

Your decision-making skills are at a new level where you are on equal footing with everyone around you. You are no longer storming into a situation where you want your voice to be heard, and being the only one who has an opinion. You are now allowing others to have their voices heard and assist with making sound decisions.

Self-Esteem

Being more self-aware has helped you grow in confidence. Your ability to acknowledge your shortcomings and weaknesses has given you the much-needed boost you needed. You are more confident in yourself. You believe in yourself and you see yourself in a way you never have before. Your self-esteem has been multiplied by believing in yourself.

Accepting and Embracing Your Self-Awareness

It is very easy to get lost or sidetracked in this day and age. We run around like headless chickens trying to do a hundred tasks in an hour before moving on to the next task. This is when we lose focus on who we are and what our purpose in life is. Before you lose yourself even more, stop and take a look around. Refer to your notebook or journal and re-read your list of goals. Re-evaluate the path you are on. Ensure that you are where you wanted to be and that you have not fallen into the trap of reverting back to the expectations of society.

If you have reverted to your old comfort zone, shake yourself loose and start over. Make a new list of goals. Block out outside influences trying to force you into believing what others dictate. Always remember that you are allowed to have your own opinions and thoughts because you have the freedom to do so.

In wrapping up this chapter, I would like to help you boost your self-awareness, and get you to where you were before you got lost. Veering off the path is not a sign of weakness, you are human after all!

The Importance of Self-Care

I realize that this might seem like a selfish move, but you have to take care of yourself before you can help others. In a world where mental and physical health are hot topics of conversation, you need to make time to refresh, recharge the internal batteries, and take care of yourself before falling down the rabbit hole. Your health and wellbeing are important to everyone you come in contact with.

Listen to Your Gut

If you have a bad feeling about something, then you know you should not be doing whatever it is. That little voice, which we have spoken about previously, will not lead you astray. You might not like what that little voice is telling you, but it is trying to tell you something. As part of your self-awareness journey, you want to follow your instinct and not impulse. You do not want to end up compromising your beliefs because you ignored the voice of reason.

Be Positive

On your new life journey, you know that being positive is a daily practice. You simply cannot be positive this morning, negative this afternoon, and in-between tonight. Your positivity is what sets you apart from others, and amplifies your self-awareness. Being positive is definitely not a one-time practice, it is something that has to happen every single day, multiple times a day. Being and remaining positive, in my opinion, is one of the most difficult tasks ever.

Self-awareness is a trait—or maybe 'practice' is the more accurate way to put it— that everyone can always improve at. It is part emotional intelligence, part perceptiveness, part critical thinking. It means knowing your weaknesses, of course, but it also means knowing your strengths and what motivates you.

–Neil Blumenthal

Chapter 20:

I Believe in You, so You Need to

Believe in You

This point cannot be stressed enough. You should always believe in yourself. Even if friends, family, or acquaintances tell you that you are wrong for believing in something, do not doubt yourself. If you believe you can climb a mountain, you will climb that mountain because that is what you believe. Challenge yourself to try something you have never tried before because you were afraid. Your belief in yourself will conquer most of your fears. I do say most because as far as being human goes, we do like to cling to some of our residual selves.

Chapters 2 and 3 saw us exploring every bit of information we could about believing and beliefs. You dug deep and uncovered some hidden treasures you never knew about. If you did not know what beliefs were before you read this book, you were given a definition. Belief systems, what people believe in, why it matters who or what you believe in, and what you do believe in, were explored. You learned about what or who you could have put your beliefs in.

We moved on to analyzing the beliefs, which was an eye-opener to see where and how our beliefs originated and formed. I am still having trouble wrapping my head around the fact that I allowed age-old traditions, handed down from generations of family members, to hold my mind hostage for so long. Believing in Santa Claus, the Easter Bunny, the Tooth Fairy, or the multicolored unicorn is not to be taken seriously, and it is mostly for the little children to protect their innocence before they start realizing that it all fades away eventually.

Why Is Believing in Yourself so Important?

Throughout this journey, we have done a lot of reflecting, soul-searching, digging, and uncovering everything we could about believing and beliefs. Believing is not only about putting your belief in something or someone, it is about discovering more about who you are and what you are capable of. I might have already told you that I believe in you because I know that you are destined to be great. How would I know that? Because I believe in the power of positivity, and if truth be told, I believe God put this book on your radar for a reason. I do not know why He would do that, but I do not ask many questions when something happens that I cannot explain. It is a matter of having faith in what cannot be explained.

Who Is Going to Believe in You if You Do Not Believe in Yourself?

If you want to succeed in life, you need to believe in yourself. You might have other people who believe in you, but their belief holds no weight if you do not believe you can succeed. If you are going to be negative and express your negativity, then no one will believe in you. Change your mindset. Make realistic goals. Adopt a couple of positive mantras. And believe in yourself. Once everyone around you sees how positive you are, they will feed off your positive energy and before you know it, you will be known as the person who created the global pandemic referred to as the You Believe in Yourself virus. The beauty of this virus is that you do not have to worry about wearing a mask or sanitizing your hands. This virus spreads by word of mouth.

Be Confident in Confidence

I am going to feed off the previous section and add that if you are not confident, no one else will have confidence in you. Without confidence, you are lacking in courage and without courage, you will be weak and crack the moment you are faced with your first obstacle. No one, not me or the stranger down the street, is going to tell you that you have to be confident every day. Everyone has an off day where they just do not want to be an adult or have responsibilities. We all have days like that, and it is normal. But, the sooner you pick yourself up and make your way back to your straight and narrow pathway, the better. You have not come this far to give up and go back to your old habits.

You Are Your Own Inspiration

When you work on your list of goals, whether it is a daily, weekly, monthly, or bucket list, you are not doing it with family, friends, or acquaintances. Your list of goals is personal to you. When you cross off an item on your list of goals, you are proud of yourself. You were the inspiration behind the goals, and you will be the inspiration behind many other goals. Remember, keep your goals realistic and achievable. If you want some long-term goals, add them to your bucket list and work towards them. Whenever you achieve a goal, reward yourself. Do something you have never done before, reach for the stars. Again, I believe in you and I also believe that you will be an inspiration to many people who will cross your path.

You Failed: Every Cloud Has a Silver Lining

One of my favorite sayings is "every cloud has a silver lining" and I remember quite a few years back, I heard a lady saying the exact quote, except she added something on that makes me think: "every cloud has a silver lining, but you should not go searching for that silver lining. If you are going to search, you might be fooled. The silver-lined cloud will show itself to you when the time is right." That made me think and realize that the lady was right. When you want something to be there, you imagine it to appear when you want it to. If you exercise patience, you will be rewarded. That is how life should be. Accidents, or in this instance a minor setback in your life journey are not intentional. The setback happened for a reason. Maybe it was to make sure you stayed true to yourself, or maybe it was to clear the path for something bigger and better. You have a choice. You can throw yourself down on the ground and be like a two-year-old having a meltdown. You can kick and scream. Or, you can remain calm, take a step back and assess the situation. Always remember, for every problem, there is a solution. The solution will present itself when the time is right.

Once Upon A Time

As you know by now, I love sharing inspirational stories. Every story I have shared since the Introduction until now, and everything in between, has been meaningful and heartfelt. Many of the people I spoke to were afraid of being judged because of their circumstances, others were afraid of being labeled as being pretentious and looking for attention. As you might recall, I did mention that there is no place for bullying and judgment here. Every single person has a right to enjoy a piece of ground on this earth, soaking up the sun, and breathing in the air that is gifted to us daily.

I wanted to end this chapter with a testimonial about a little boy that has wormed his way into the hearts of many people from all across the world. The story will be told from an outsider's point of view. Please note, this is a real-life story of faith, love, hope, trust, and belief as told by Jayme Bella.

This is a story about a little boy named Reef Carneson. As I am sharing his testimony, Reef is fighting for his life. Reef was born in Johannesburg, South Africa in September 2009. At the age of five months, Reef was diagnosed with acute lymphoblastic leukemia. Before he turned a year old, Reef had a bone marrow transplant. At the time, Reef was the youngest bone marrow recipient in South Africa.

The bone marrow transplant was a success, but unfortunately, complications crept in and Reef was diagnosed with graft-versus-host disease (GVHD) that affected most of the organs in his body. The condition was so severe that Reef could not walk, talk, cry, or eat, and he was fed via a gastric tube. Reef's parents, Ryan and Lydia, researched Reef's condition to see if there were any treatment plans. They found a hospital, the Children's Hospital of Los Angeles, who agreed to treat Reef. The family, along with members of both families and friends, began fundraising to get the funds needed to get Reef to Los Angeles as soon as possible.

In 2011, Ryan, Lydia, Reef, and Peyton (their young daughter) started their journey across the Atlantic Ocean. Once there and settled in, treatment began and Reef started responding to the treatment. He started walking, eating on his own, and communicating with his family. Unfortunately, GVHD is not a very forgiving disease and has had lasting effects on Reef's speech, joints, skin, and eyes. Throughout Reef's time in Los Angeles, Lydia inspired people by sharing her son with the world and encouraging people to have hope and believe by praying. Watching Reef grow up has been a privilege that I will treasure for the rest of my life.

Reaching the end of their treatment plan in Los Angeles, they transferred to the Cincinnati Children's Hospital in Ohio. In addition to the GVHD, the family was told that Reef had developed skin cancer on his head! It was during this time that Reef's beloved grandfather was also diagnosed with skin cancer on his arm (grandfather passed away in 2020). Sadly, the Carneson's medical visa was expiring after more than nine years and they were forced to pack up their family and either move back to South Africa or move to the United Kingdom. They opted for the United Kingdom.

At the end of April 2021, Reef's health took a drastic turn. After more biopsies and scans, Reef was diagnosed with lung cancer. At the age of 12, this little boy has been to hell and back, but he keeps on fighting. The doctors told Lydia and Ryan that they gather their family before Reef leaves this earth to be with his beloved grandfather. Family flew in from South Africa, the United States, and even those in the United Kingdom came to be with Reef.

The family has been inundated with messages of faith, hope, and belief, including prayers. But unfortunately, some people do not believe the way others do, and they do not see Reef ever recovering. They have been condemning Lydia and Ryan for "torturing" Reef and some even went as far as to say that they should let him die. I will never be able to understand why people have to be so mean. Reef has told his parents he knows he is going to heaven to be with his grandfather, but he is not ready to go just yet.

This is a story about a little boy that showed millions of people how to come together and be united in prayer. He showed people how to have faith and hope. Reef showed people that if you believe in yourself, anything is possible. Reef has inspired more people than he will know. Until Reef takes his last breath, we will keep on believing that God is not ready to take him home just yet (About Reef, n.d.).

Conclusion

We have reached the part of the book where you are either ecstatic to see it come to an end, or wishing it could go on a little more. Whatever the case may be, our journey together has reached the final destination and we have to go our separate ways now. I would like to thank you for embarking on this journey of self-discovery with me. It has most definitely been an epic journey filled with so much information.

My biggest hope is that the knowledge you have gained throughout this journey will help you in areas of your life where you have been struggling. Even though our time together is coming to an end, I want you to know that you will always have me in the palm of your hand should you need a refresher. The scenarios that are interspersed throughout this book can be amended to suit any situation. The most important key takeaway I wish for you to take with you on your new journey is that you never stop believing in yourself. You do not have to believe in anyone or anything if you do not want to but believe in yourself.

If you enjoyed this book and found it helped you find yourself, please consider leaving a review on Amazon. If you have any questions or suggestions regarding anything mentioned in this book, please leave a comment in the review section. The book is all about being positive and enforcing energy for all who read it. Please consider the feelings of others, and refrain from being judgmental and nasty.

The Last Word

During our journey through life, we will encounter many obstacles to get to our destination. The biggest goal is finding yourself and believing that you are on this particular path for a reason. You are unique. You were hand-crafted with love and adoration. You are on this earth to touch the lives of others and to make a positive impact on the lives of people you meet.

Thank you for joining me on this epic journey. May God send angels to watch over you and keep you safe as you navigate your way through life. Go in faith dear friends. Amen.

References

A Conscious Rethink. (n.d.). *20 Things you really ought to believe if.* A Conscious Rethink. https://www.aconsciousrethink.com/12817/things-to-believe-in/

A quote by Mahatma Gandhi. (n.d.). Goodreads.com. https://www.goodreads.com/quotes/50584-your-beliefs-become-your-thoughts-your-thoughts-become-your-words

About Reef. (n.d.). Reef. https://www.savebabyreef.com/about-reef

Ackerman, C. (2019, July 3). *What is self-awareness and why is it important? [+5 Ways to increase it].* PositivePsychology.com. https://positivepsychology.com/self-awareness-matters-how-you-can-be-more-self-aware/

Andreas. (n.d.). *24 Important pros & cons of dieting.* E&C. https://environmental-conscience.com/dieting-pros-cons/

Az Quotes. (n.d.). *Shusaku Endo Quote.* A-Z Quotes. https://www.azquotes.com/quote/462480

Ballard, J. (2020, December 23). *Exercising and sticking to a healthy diet are the most common 2021 New Year's resolutions | YouGov.* Today.yougov.com. https://today.yougov.com/topics/lifestyle/articles-reports/2020/12/23/2021-new-years-resolutions-poll

Belli, G. (2018, February 18). *5 Disadvantages of doing what you love.* PayScale. https://www.payscale.com/career-news/2018/02/5-disadvantages-love

Brainy Quote. (n.d.-a). *Alfred Lord Tennyson Quotes*. BrainyQuote. https://www.brainyquote.com/quotes/alfred_lord_tennyson_153702

Brainy Quote. (n.d.-b). *Babe Ruth Quotes*. BrainyQuote. https://www.brainyquote.com/quotes/babe_ruth_130004

Brown, L. (2017, December 8). *Here are 7 unusual signs you're becoming the person you were meant to be*. Hack Spirit. https://hackspirit.com/7-unusual-signs-youre-becoming-person-meant/

Burriston, N. (2020, August 27). *5 Types of mistakes that can transform your life*. Medium. https://medium.com/age-of-awareness/5-types-of-mistakes-that-can-transform-your-life-7d92ca7c9a71

Cambridge *Dictionary*. (n.d.). MANIPULATION | meaning in the Cambridge English Dictionary. Cambridge.org. https://dictionary.cambridge.org/dictionary/english/manipulation

Casano, T. (2015, June 25). *10 Ways to believe in yourself again when life gets rough*. Lifehack; Lifehack. https://www.lifehack.org/288536/10-ways-believe-yourself-again

CDC. (2017, March 2). *CDC - How much sleep do I need? - Sleep and sleep disorders*. CDC. https://www.cdc.gov/sleep/about_sleep/how_much_sleep.html

Charlotte, J. (2014, April 3). *Living in the past? 7 Ways to let go and live a happy life*. Lifehack. https://www.lifehack.org/articles/communication/7-ways-let-the-past-and-live-happy-life.html

Cirino, E. (2018, July 19). *6 Ways to Build Trust in Yourself*. Healthline. https://www.healthline.com/health/trusting-yourself

Craig Groeschel Quotes. (n.d.). Quotefancy.com. https://quotefancy.com/craig-groeschel-quotes

Daum, K. (2015, October 5). *7 Ways to apply your personal core values in daily life.* Inc.com. https://www.inc.com/kevin-daum/7-ways-to-apply-your-personal-core-values-in-daily-life.html

Direct Recruiters Inc. (n.d.). *Working remotely has advantages & disadvantages...Is it right for you?* Direct Recruiters Inc. https://www.directrecruiters.com/dri-candidate-advice/working-remotely-advantages-disadvantages-right/

Exeter, K. (n.d.). *8 ways to rebuild lost confidence | Kelly Exeter.* Kellyexeter.com.au. https://kellyexeter.com.au/how-to-rebuild-lost-confidence

Foley, L. (2020, September 11). *Why do we need sleep?* Sleep Foundation. https://www.sleepfoundation.org/how-sleep-works/why-do-we-need-sleep

Gaille, B. (2015, August 25). *12 Pros and cons of emotional intelligence.* BrandonGaille.com. https://brandongaille.com/12-pros-and-cons-of-emotional-intelligence/

Get enough sleep - MyHealthfinder | health.gov. (2020, October 15). Health.gov. https://health.gov/myhealthfinder/topics/everyday-healthy-living/mental-health-and-relationships/get-enough-sleep#panel-2

Gliatto, M. (2020, December 29). *Positive and negative effects of religion.* Medium. https://medium.com/illumination/positive-and-negative-effects-of-religion-7ec841feef07

Greenfield, B. (2011, September 21). *Top 10 reasons exercise is bad for you.* Trainingpeaks.com; TrainingPeaks.

https://www.trainingpeaks.com/blog/top-10-reasons-exercise-is-bad-for-you/

Gregoire, C. (2018, February 8). *How money changes the way you think and feel.* Greater Good. https://greatergood.berkeley.edu/article/item/how_money_changes_the_way_you_think_and_feel

Guidance, T. F., & Center, T. (2020, July 17). *What do I believe in and why does it matter? | Family Guidance & Therapy Center.* Familyguidanceandtherapy.com. https://familyguidanceandtherapy.com/what-do-i-believe-in-and-why-does-it-matter/

health.gov. (n.d.). *USDA dietary guidelines final - DGA2000.pdf.* https://health.gov/sites/default/files/2020-01/DGA2000.pdf

History.com Editors. (2018a, January 5). *Judaism.* HISTORY; A&E Television Networks. https://www.history.com/topics/religion/judaism

History.com Editors. (2018b, August 21). *Christianity.* HISTORY; A&E Television Networks. https://www.history.com/topics/religion/history-of-christianity

History.com Editors. (2018c, August 21). *Islam.* HISTORY; A&E Television Networks. https://www.history.com/topics/religion/islam

Ho, L. (2021, April 19). *20 Personal SMART goals examples to improve your life.* https://www.lifehack.org/864427/examples-of-personal-smart-goals

Hope Grows Editor. (2019, April 29). *Why Memory matters for all of us | Benefits of having a good memory.* Hope Grows.

https://hopegrows.net/news/why-having-a-good-memory-matters

How to believe in yourself and build self-confidence. (n.d.). Skilledatlife.com. http://www.skilledatlife.com/how-to-believe-in-yourself-and-build-self-confidence/

Huddleston Jr, T. (2021, January 21). *Mega Millions is up to $970 million—there's one way to up the odds of winning, according to a Harvard statistics professor.* CNBC. https://www.cnbc.com/2021/01/21/how-to-up-the-odds-of-winning-a-lottery-harvard-professor.html

Jennifer. (n.d.). *10 Benefits of self awareness and how it can impact your life | Contentment Questing.* Contentment Questing. https://contentmentquesting.com/benefits-of-self-awareness/

Joan D. Chittister Quote: *"Indifference is the acid of life. It erodes all the spirit that's in us and makes us useless to anyone else. We all have..."* (n.d.). Quotefancy.com. https://quotefancy.com/quote/1521624/Joan-D-Chittister-Indifference-is-the-acid-of-life-It-erodes-all-the-spirit-that-s-in-us

Justesen, D. (2019, July 22). *10 Sure signs you're making the right decisions.* Medium. https://medium.com/the-ascent/10-sure-signs-youre-making-the-right-decisions-22061d2c5624

Kirby, S. (2021, May 5). *9 Ways love is powerful | Betterhelp.* Www.betterhelp.com. https://www.betterhelp.com/advice/love/9-ways-love-is-powerful/

Leech, J. (2020, February 24). *10 Reasons why good sleep is important.* Healthline. https://www.healthline.com/nutrition/10-reasons-why-good-sleep-is-important

M, K. (2017, October 31). *Trust in relationship: Why is it important and how to build it?* MomJunction. https://www.momjunction.com/articles/trust-in-relationship_00434595/#TrustInRelationship1

Manly, C. M. (2019, May 9). *5 Daily strategies for boosting self-awareness the self-compassion.* Dr. Carla Manly, PhD. https://drcarlamanly.com/self-compassion-self-awareness/

Mark Victor Hansen. (n.d.). *6 Tips to create a balanced life.* SUCCESS. https://www.success.com/6-tips-to-create-a-balanced-life/

Mead, J. (2013, October 2). *10 Powerful beliefs that will transform your life.* Business Insider. https://www.businessinsider.com/10-beliefs-that-make-your-life-awesome-2013-10?IR=T

Merriam Webster. (n.d.). *Definition of SLEEP.* Merriam-Webster.com. https://www.merriam-webster.com/dictionary/sleep

Merriam-Webster. (n.d.-a). *Definition of BELIEF.* Merriam-Webster.com. https://www.merriam-webster.com/dictionary/belief

Merriam-Webster. (n.d.-b). *Definition of DIET.* Merriam-Webster.com. https://www.merriam-webster.com/dictionary/diet

Merriam-Webster. (n.d.-c). *Definition of FUNDAMENTALIST.* Www.merriam-Webster.com. https://www.merriam-webster.com/dictionary/fundamentalist

Merriam-Webster. (n.d.-d). *Definition of RELIGION.* Merriam-Webster.com. https://www.merriam-webster.com/dictionary/religion

Merriam-Webster. (n.d.). *Definition of ADDICTION.* Merriam-Webster.com. https://www.merriam-webster.com/dictionary/addiction

Molla, R. (2019, October 9). *Working remotely: the pros and cons of working from home.* Vox; Vox. https://www.vox.com/recode/2019/10/9/20885699/remote-work-from-anywhere-change-coworking-office-real-estate

Morin, A. (2018, November 27). *10 Signs you're a mentally strong person (Even though most people think these are weaknesses).* Inc.com; Inc. https://www.inc.com/amy-morin/10-signs-youre-a-mentally-strong-person-even-though-most-people-think-these-are-weaknesses.html

Neil Blumenthal Quotes. (n.d.). BrainyQuote. https://www.brainyquote.com/quotes/neil_blumenthal_927656?src=t_self-awareness

Nemko, M. (2014, March 16). *Is Status-Seeking Worth it? | Psychology Today.* Www.psychologytoday.com. https://www.psychologytoday.com/intl/blog/how-do-life/201403/is-status-seeking-worth-it

New King James Version. (1982). Bible Gateway. https://www.biblegateway.com/versions/New-King-James-Version-NKJV-Bible/#booklist

Newsom, R. (2020, November 3). How blue light affects sleep. Sleep Foundation. https://www.sleepfoundation.org/bedroom-environment/blue-light

Oskar Nowik. (2015, June 9). *7 Powerful reasons why you should believe in yourself.* Lifehack; Lifehack. https://www.lifehack.org/articles/communication/7-powerful-reasons-why-you-should-believe-yourself.html

Osmun, R. (2015, July 21). *Oversleeping: The effects & health risks of sleeping too much.* Amerisleep Blog; Amerisleep. https://amerisleep.com/blog/oversleeping-the-health-effects/

Pacheco, D. (2020, December 1). *Sleep disorders | National Sleep Foundation.* Sleepfoundation.org. https://www.sleepfoundation.org/sleep-disorders

Physiopedia. (n.d.). *Personal values and beliefs.* Physiopedia. https://www.physio-pedia.com/Personal_Values_and_Beliefs

R, J. (2016, July 6). *16 Habit changes you can make to live a better life.* Baba-Mail. https://www.ba-bamail.com/content.aspx?emailid=21560

Rakoczy, C. (2019, April 2). *Why money is important: Benefits, downsides, and more | LendEDU.* LendEDU. https://lendedu.com/blog/why-money-is-important/

Reddy, K. (2015, May 12). *Working in an office: 14 Advantages and disadvantages.* WiseStep. https://content.wisestep.com/advantages-and-disadvantages-of-working-in-an-office/

Savage, C. (n.d.). *You are important! Here's 6 reasons why.* Reliable Life Strategies. https://reliablelifestrategies.com/you-are-important/

Schreiber, K. (2016, February 10). *How to make better decisions.* Greatist. https://greatist.com/live/decision-making-signs

Seetubtim, M. (2014, December 15). *How do you know when something is right?* HuffPost. https://www.huffpost.com/entry/how-do-you-know-when-some_1_b_6279696

Sharma, A. (2014, January 31). *Major advantages and disadvantages of habit formation.* Psychology Discussion - Discuss Anything about Psychology. https://www.psychologydiscussion.net/habit/major-advantages-and-disadvantages-of-habit-formation/636

Simple English Wikipedia. (n.d.). *List of religions - Simple English Wikipedia, the free encyclopedia.* Wikipedia.org. https://simple.wikipedia.org/wiki/List_of_religions

Skindzier, J. (n.d.). *Status matters - And wealth doesn't guarantee it.* AskMen. https://www.askmen.com/dating/curtsmith_300/389_why-status-matters.html

Stigall, A. (2018, November 28). *How to know when you're worshipping your work.* NewSpring.cc. https://newspring.cc/articles/how-to-know-when-youre-worshipping-your-work

Svoboda, E. (2019, April 3). *What happens when we seek status instead of goodness?* Greater Good. https://greatergood.berkeley.edu/article/item/What_Happens_When_We_Seek_Status_Instead_of_Goodness

T, M. (2017, May 4). *7 Basic human needs according to Maslow - Survival Report.* Survival Report. https://survivalreport.org/basic-human-needs/

Tripp, P. D. (2019, July 6). *5 Dangers of Money.* Www.crossway.org. https://www.crossway.org/articles/5-dangers-of-money/

Usó-Doménech, J. L., & Nescolarde-Selva, J. (2015). *What are belief systems? Foundations of Science, 21(1),* 147–152. https://doi.org/10.1007/s10699-015-9409-z

Waxman, O. B. (2019, July 15). *Lots of people have theories about Neil Armstrong's "One Small Step for Man" Quote. Here's what we really know.* Time; Time. https://time.com/5621999/neil-armstrong-quote/

Webster University. (n.d.). *LibGuides: Holidays and observances: Islam.* Webster.edu. https://libguides.webster.edu/holidays/islam

What is the sin of gluttony? Its definition and consequences. (n.d.). Christianity.com.

https://www.christianity.com/wiki/sin/what-is-the-sin-of-gluttony-its-definition-and-consequences.html

Wikipedia Contributors. (2019a, February 12). *Mosque*. Wikipedia; Wikimedia Foundation. https://en.wikipedia.org/wiki/Mosque

Wikipedia Contributors. (2019b, May 13). *Gluttony*. Wikipedia; Wikimedia Foundation. https://en.wikipedia.org/wiki/Gluttony

Writer, G. (n.d.). *15 Simple ways to get confidence back*. Lifehack. https://www.lifehack.org/articles/communication/15-simple-ways-get-confidence-back.html

Zavada, J. (2020, May 11). *Explore 4 different types of love in the Bible*. Learn Religions. https://www.learnreligions.com/types-of-love-in-the-bible-700177